FICTION HOUSE PRESS
PRESENTS

SPACE SCIENCE FICTION

May 1952
Vol. 1 No. 1

This reprint edition is a facsimile of the original digest magazine. Variations in printing and quality can be attributed to the original magazine which was printed on rough woodpulp paper. No attempt has been made to politically correct any language deemed inappropriate to the modern reader.

ISBN 978-1-64720-558-4

www.FictionHousePress.com
fictionhousepress@gmail.com

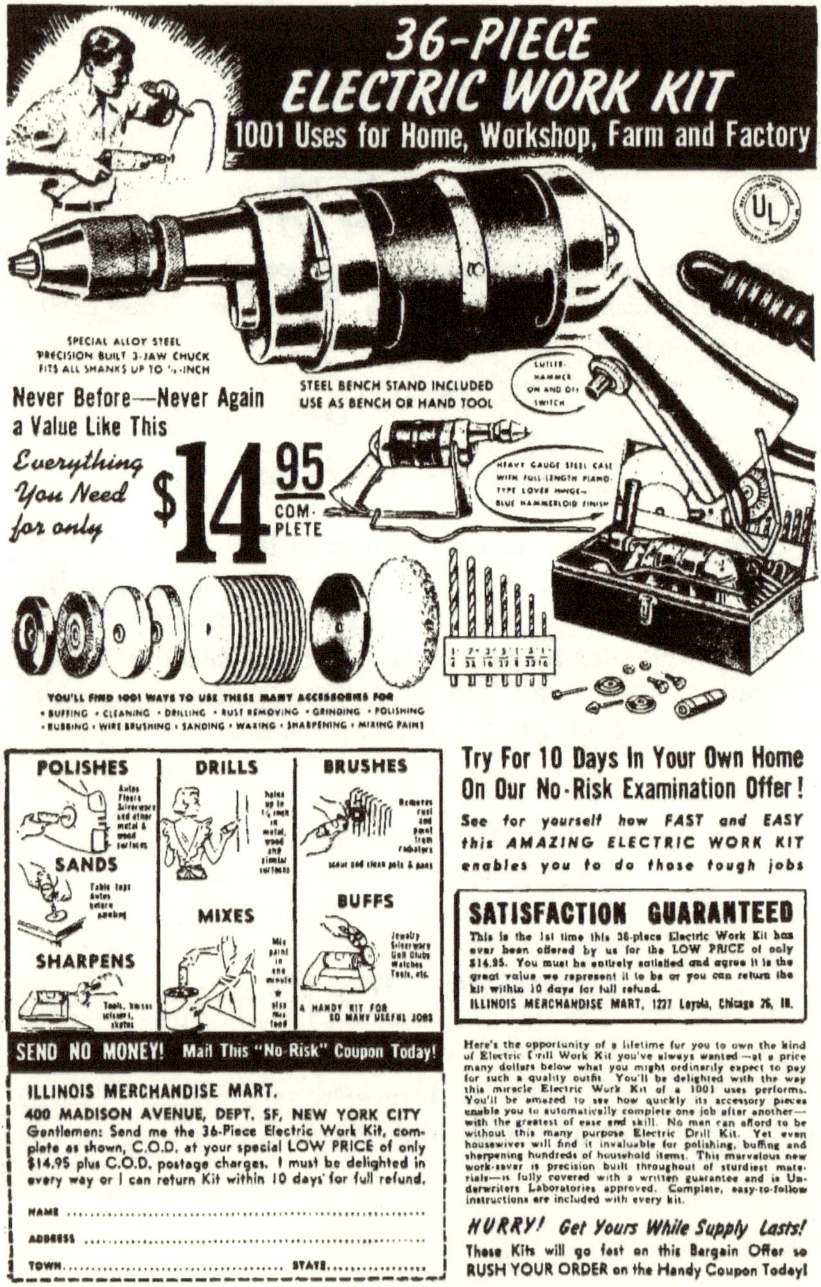

36-PIECE ELECTRIC WORK KIT

1001 Uses for Home, Workshop, Farm and Factory

SPECIAL ALLOY STEEL PRECISION BUILT 3-JAW CHUCK FITS ALL SHANKS UP TO ¼-INCH

STEEL BENCH STAND INCLUDED USE AS BENCH OR HAND TOOL

CUTLER-HAMMER ON AND OFF SWITCH

HEAVY GAUGE STEEL CASE WITH FULL-LENGTH PIANO-TYPE COVER HINGE—BLUE HAMMERLOID FINISH

Never Before—Never Again a Value Like This

Everything You Need for only **$14.95 COMPLETE**

YOU'LL FIND 1001 WAYS TO USE THESE MANY ACCESSORIES FOR
• BUFFING • CLEANING • DRILLING • RUST REMOVING • GRINDING • POLISHING
• RUBBING • WIRE BRUSHING • SANDING • WAXING • SHARPENING • MIXING PAINT

Try For 10 Days In Your Own Home On Our No-Risk Examination Offer!

See for yourself how FAST and EASY this AMAZING ELECTRIC WORK KIT enables you to do those tough jobs

SATISFACTION GUARANTEED

This is the 1st time this 36-piece Electric Work Kit has ever been offered by us for the LOW PRICE of only $14.95. You must be entirely satisfied and agree it is the great value we represent it to be or you can return the kit within 10 days for full refund.

ILLINOIS MERCHANDISE MART, 1227 Loyola, Chicago 26, Ill.

Here's the opportunity of a lifetime for you to own the kind of Electric Drill Work Kit you've always wanted—at a price many dollars below what you might ordinarily expect to pay for such a quality outfit. You'll be delighted with the way this miracle Electric Work Kit of a 1001 uses performs. You'll be amazed to see how quickly its accessory pieces enable you to automatically complete one job after another—with the greatest of ease and skill. No man can afford to be without this many purpose Electric Drill Kit. Yet even housewives will find it invaluable for polishing, buffing and sharpening hundreds of household items. This marvelous new work-saver is precision built throughout of sturdiest materials—is fully covered with a written guarantee and is Underwriters Laboratories approved. Complete, easy-to-follow instructions are included with every kit.

HURRY! Get Yours While Supply Lasts!

These Kits will go fast on this Bargain Offer so RUSH YOUR ORDER on the Handy Coupon Today!

SPACE SCIENCE FICTION

MAY, 1952 Vol. 1, No. 1

FEATURE NOVEL

NOVELETTES

SHORT STORIES

REVIEW

DEPARTMENTS

COVER BY ORBAN

Illustrations by Orban, Schecterson, Harrison

JOHN RAYMOND • *Publisher*
BILL BRADLEY • *Circulation Mgr.*
DAVID GELLER • *Advertising Mgr.*
LESTER DEL REY • *Editor*
BEN PETERS • *Assoc. Editor*
MILTON BERWIN • *Art Director*
West Coast Office • H. L. MITCHELL

SPACE SCIENCE FICTION is published bi-monthly by Space Publications, Inc., 175 Fifth Avenue, New York 10, N. Y. Copyright 1952 by Space Publications, Inc. Entry as second-class matter applied for at the Post Office, at New York, N. Y. Subscriptions $2.00 per year in the United States and Possessions; $2.50 per year in Canada; $3.00 elsewhere. All subscripions should be addressed to Space Publications, Inc., 175 Fifth Ave., New York 10, N. Y. Not responsible for unsolicited manuscripts or art work. All submissions must include return postage.

$2.00 per year in U. S. A. PRINTED IN THE U. S. A. 35¢ per copy

 178

EDITORIAL

FIRST FLIGHT

THE first issue of a magazine is something like a new baby. Behind it lie months of worry and anticipation; ahead lies a period of growth and development toward its own position in the world. But even now, while it may resemble others to some extent, it is unique and with a personality of its own. Its name must reflect that.

SPACE SCIENCE FICTION seems the most appropriate name that a science fiction magazine could have. From the very first appearance of stories dealing with science and the future, space travel has been one of the most popular themes, and it continues to grow in favor with every year.

We like good space fiction, and we intend to bring you the best of it. Nothing is more welcome than a good story of man's conquest of this final frontier. The space-opera of flashing rayguns and invincible heroes has long since been overdone, but there are as many stories to be written of man against space as there are worlds out there waiting for us. We'd like to explore every one of those possible worlds to meet every challenge that can arise in our efforts to spread throughout the universe.

However, **SPACE** isn't a title which restricts us to a monotonous diet of a single type of story. Webster's New Collegiate Dictionary defines **SPACE** as: *That which is characterized by extension in all directions, boundlessness, and indefinite divisibility.* This is broad enough a definition to cover all the possible futures and ideas that man can invent.

Time travel, robots, biological mutations, or sociological conflicts are only a few of the possible extensions in all directions which we want to follow. Even an occasional fantasy which deals with some world of possibility beyond what we now know or believe will be welcome. And there are still countless fine stories to be written about this planet and the near future.

Our sole aim will be to bring you a varied selection of first-rate fiction, and our only taboo will be against dullness. We don't intend to make claims that this is or will be *the* best science fiction magazine; that's a matter of taste, and every magazine will be "best" to some group of readers. We don't intend to claim it is the most mature magazine, either, until we find a better definition for maturity. We *do* intend to make this the best magazine our honest efforts can give you, and to make sure that it lives up to the purpose of all good fiction—suspenseful, stimulating entertainment.

Inevitably, a first issue can never do everything that we want the magazine to do. It will take the help of the readers to guide us toward the ideal we have in mind. We want your suggestions and your objections. We need your praise when we have earned it, and we'll expect your criticism when it is merited. Science fiction has always been a cooperative concern, and we hope it always will be.

This applies to everything—the stories, the writers, the artists, covers, format—including your opinion of this editorial and the editor, if you like.

We also want to know what features you'd like to see. At present, we're planning to run a letter section for those who write in; we need your letters for that, though we want to hear from you, even if you ask us not to print your letter.

We'll have reviews of the best of the new books—and some of the old that deserve special mention. We expect to bring you news of stories to come, and the results on stories that have appeared. We plan to use occasional articles—but only when they are of special interest to science fiction readers, rather than as a regular feature. And we're planning to keep our future editorials devoted to those aspects of science fiction which we feel have been neglected, instead of simply boosting our own stock.

But you know better than we can what you like—and we want to learn exactly what that is. Let's hear from you!

LESTER DEL REY.

PURSUIT *by* LESTER DEL REY

Illustrated by ORBAN

I

FEAR cut through the unconscious mind of Wilbur Hawkes. With almost physical violence, it tightened his throat and knifed at his heart. It darted into his numbed brain, screaming at him.

He was a soft egg in a vast globe of elastic gelatine. Two creatures swam menacingly through the resisting globe toward him. The gelatine fought against them, but they came on. One was near, and made a mystic pass. He screamed at it, and the gelatine grew stronger, throwing them back and away. Suddenly, the creatures drew back. A door opened, and they were gone. But he couldn't let them go. If they escaped . . .

Hawkes jerked upright in his bed, gasping out a hoarse cry, and the sound of his own voice completed the awakening. He opened his eyes to a murky darkness that was barely relieved by the little night-light. For a second, the nightmare was so strong on his mind that he seemed to see two shadows beyond the door, rushing down the steps. He fought off the illusion, and with straining senses jerked his head around the room. There was nothing there.

Sweat was beading his forehead, and he could feel his pulse racing. He had to get out—had to leave—at once!

He forced the idea aside. There was something cloudy in his mind, but he made reason take over and shove away some of the heavy fear. His fingers found a cigarette and lighted it automatically. The first familiar breath of smoke in his lungs helped. He drew in deeply again, while the tiny sounds in the room became meaningful. There was the insistent ticking of a clock and the soft shushing sound of a tape recorder. He stared at the machine, running on fast rewind, and reversed it to play. But the tape seemed to be blank, or erased.

He crushed the cigarette out on a table-top where other butts lay in disorder. It looked wrong, and his mind leaped up in sudden frantic fear, before he could calm it again. This time. reason echoed his emotional unease.

Hawkes had never smoked before!

But his fingers were already lighting another by old habit. His thoughts lurched, seeking for an answer. There was only a vague sense of something missing—a period of time seemed to have passed. It felt like a long period, but he had no memory of it. There had been the final fight with Irma, when he'd gone stalking out of the house, telling her to get a divorce any way she wanted. He'd opened the mail-box and taken out a letter—a letter from a Professor . . .

His mind refused to go further. There was only a complete blank after that. But it had been in midwinter, and now he could make out the faint outlines of full-leafed trees against the sky through the window! Months had gone by—and there was no faintest trace of them in his mind.

They'll get you! You can't escape! Hurry, go, GO! . . .

The cigarette fell from his shaking hands, and he was half out of the bed before the rational part of his mind could cut off the fear thoughts. He flipped on the lights, afraid of the dimness. It didn't help The room was dusty, as if unused for months, and there was a cobweb in one corner by the mirror.

His own face shocked him. It was the same lean, sharp-featured face as ever, under the shock of nondescript, sandy hair. His ears still stuck out too much, and his lips were a trifle too thin. It looked no more than his thirty years; but it was a strained face, now—painted with weeks of fatigue, and grayish with fear, sweat-streaked and with nervous tension in every corded tendon of his throat. His somewhat bony, average-height figure shook visibly as he climbed from the bed.

Hawkes stood fighting himself, trying to get back in the bed, but it was a losing battle. Something seemed to swing up in the corner of the room, as if a shadow moved. He jerked his head toward it, but there was nothing there.

He heard his breath gasping harshly, and his knuckles whitened. There was the taste of blood in the corner of his mouth where he was biting his lips.

Get out! They'll be here at once! Leave—GO!

HIS hands were already fumbling with his underclothing. He drew on briefs jerkily, and grabbed for the shirt and suit he had never seen before. He was no longer thinking, now. Blind panic was winning. He thrust his feet into shoes, not bothering with socks.

A slip of paper fell from his coat, with big sprawled Greek letters. He saw only the last line as it fell to the floor—some equation that ended with an infinity sign. Then psi and alpha, connected by a dash. The alpha sign had been scratched out, and something written over it. He tried to reach it, and more papers spilled from his coat pocket. The fear washed up more strongly. He forgot the papers. Even the cigarettes were too far away for him to return to them. His wallet lay on the chair, and he barely grabbed it before the urge overpowered him completely.

The doorknob slipped in his sweating hands, but he managed to turn it. The elevator wasn't at his floor, and he couldn't stop for it. His feet pounded on the stairs, taking him down the three floors to the street at a breakneck pace. The walls of the stairway seemed to be rushing together, as if trying to close the way. He screamed at them, until they were behind, and he was charging out of the front door.

A half-drunken couple was coming in—a fat, older man and a slim girl he barely saw. He hit them, throwing them aside. He jerked from the entrance. Cars were streaming down West End Avenue. He dashed across, paying no attention to them. His rush carried him onto the opposite sidewalk. Then, finally, the blind panic left him, and he was leaning against a building, gasping for breath, and wondering whether his heart could endure the next beat.

Across the street, the fat man he had hit was coming after him. Hawkes gathered himself together to apologize, but the words never came. A second blinding horror hit at him, and his eyes darted up towards the windows of his apartment.

It was only a tiny glow, at first, like a drop from the heart of a sun. Then, before he could more than blink, it spread, until the whole apartment seemed to blaze. A gout of smoke poured from the shattering window, and a dull concussion struck his ears.

The infernally bright flame flickered, leaped outward from the window, and died down almost as quickly as it had come, leaving twisted, half-molten metal where the window frames had been.

They'd almost gotten him! Hawkes felt his legs weaken and quiver, while his eyes remained glued to the spot that had lighted the whole street a second before. They'd tried —but he'd escaped in time.

It must have been a thermite bomb—nothing but thermite could be that hot. He had never imagined that even such a bomb could give so much heat so quickly. Where? In the tape-recorder?

He waited numbly, expecting more fire, but the brief flame seemed to have died out completely. He shook his head, unbelieving, and started to cross the street again, to survey the damage or to join the crowd that was beginning to collect.

THE fear surged up in him again, halting his step as if he'd struck a physical barrier. With it came the sound of an auto-horn, the button held down permanently. His eyes darted down the street, to see a long, gray sedan with old-fashioned running-boards come around the corner on two wheels. Its brakes screeched, and it skidded to a halt beside Hawkes' apartment building.

A slim young man in gray tweeds leaped out of it and came to a stop. He threw back heavy black hair with a toss of his head and ran into the crowd that parted to let him through. Someone began pointing towards Hawkes.

Hawkes tried to slide around the corner without being seen, but a flashlight in the young man's hands pinpointed him. A yell went up.

"There he goes!"

His feet sounded hopelessly on the sidewalk as he dashed up toward Broadway, but behind came the sound of others in pursuit, and the shouting was becoming a meaningless babble as others took it up. There was no longer any doubt. Someone was certainly after him—there'd been no time to turn in an alarm over the fire in his apartment. They'd been coming for him before that started.

What hideous crime could he have committed during the period he couldn't remember? Or what spy-ring had encircled him?

He had no time to think of the questions, even. He ducked into the thin swarm of a few people leaving a theater just as the pursuing group rounded the corner, with the slim young man in the lead.

Their cries were enough. Hands reached for him from the theater crowd, and a foot stretched out to trip him up. Terror lent speed to his legs, but he could never outdistance them, as long as others picked up the chase.

A sudden blast of heat struck down, and the air was golden and hazy above him. He staggered sideways, blinded by the glare. The crowd was screaming in fear now, no longer holding him back. He felt the edge of a subway entrance. There was no other choice. He ducked down the steps, while his vision slowly returned, and risked a glance back at the street—just as the whole entrance came down in a wreck of broken wood and metal.

A clap of thundering noise sounded above him, drowning the hoarse screams of the people. The few persons in the station rushed for the fallen entrance, to mill about it crazily, just as a train pulled in. Hawkes started toward it, and then realized his pursuers would suspect that. Whatever frightful weapon had been used against him had backfired on them—but they'd catch him at the next stop.

HE found space at the end of the platform and dropped off, skirting behind the train, and avoiding the high-voltage rails.

The uptown platform held only three people, and they seemed to be too busy at the other end, trying to see the wreckage, to notice him. He vaulted onto it, and dashed into the men's room. The few contents of his coat pocket came out quickly, and he began to stuff them into his trousers. He shoved the coat into a garbage can, wet his hair and slicked it back, and opened his shirt collar. The change didn't make much of a disguise, but they wouldn't be expecting him to show up so near where he entered.

His skin prickled as he came out, but he fought down the sickness in his stomach. A few drops of rain were beginning to fall, and the crowd around the accident was thinning out. That might help him —or it might prove more dangerous. He had to chance it.

He stopped to buy a paper, maintaining an air of casual interest in the crowd.

"What happened?" he asked.

The newsstand attendant jerked his eyes back from the excitement reluctantly. "Damned if I know. Someone says a ball lightning came down and broke over there. Caved in the entrance. Nobody's hurt seriously, they say. I was just stacking up to go home when I heard it go off. Didn't see it. Just saw the entrance falling in."

Hawkes picked up his change and turned back across Broadway, pretending he was studying the paper. The dateline showed it was July 10, just seven months from the beginning of his memory lapse. He couldn't believe that there had been time enough for any group to invent a heat-ray, if such a thing could exist. Yet nothing else would explain the two sudden bursts of flame he had seen. Even if it could be invented, it would hardly be used in public for anything less than a National Emergency.

What had happened in the seven blanked-out months?

II

THE room was smelly and cheap, with dirty walls and no carpet on the floor, but it was a relief after the hours of tramping and riding about the city. Hawkes sat on the rickety chair, letting the wetness dry out of his clothes. He looked at the bed, trying to convince himself he could strip and warm up there while his clothes dried. But something in his head warned him that he couldn't—he'd have to be ready to run again. The same urge had made him demand a room on the ground floor, where he could escape through the window if they found him. They could never find him here—but they would! Sooner or later, whatever was after him would come!

It had seemed simple enough, before. There had been three friends he could trust. Seven months, he had felt, couldn't have killed their faith in him, no matter what he'd done. And perhaps he'd been right, though there'd been no chance to test it.

He'd almost been caught at the first place. The two men outside had seemed to be no more than a couple of friends awaiting for a bus. Only the approach of another man who resembled Hawkes had tipped him off, by the quick interest they had shown.

The other places had also been posted—and beyond the third, he'd seen the gray sedan with the running boards, parked back in the shadows, waiting.

There had been less than ten dollars in his wallet, and most of that had gone for cab fares. He'd barely had enough left for this dingy room, the later edition of the newspaper, and the coffee and donuts that lay beside him, half-consumed.

He glanced toward the door, listening with quick fear as steps sounded on the stairs. Then he drew his breath in again, and reached for the newspaper. But it told him as little as the first one had.

This one mentioned the two mysterious explosions of "ball lightning" in a feature on the first page, but only as curiosities. They even gave his address and listed the apartment as being in his name, though apparently not currently occupied. But no other reference was made to him, or to the chase.

He shook his head at that. He couldn't see a newspaperman refusing to make a story of it, if there was any other news about him to which they could tie the burning of his apartment. Apparently it was not the police who were after him, and he hadn't been guilty of anything so ordinary as murder.

OUTSIDE the window, a sudden scream sounded, and he jerked from the chair, reaching the door before he realized it was only a cat on the prowl. He shuddered, his old hatred of cats coming to the surface. For a minute, he thought of shutting the window. But he couldn't cut off his chance to retreat through the garbage-littered backyard.

He returned to his search, beginning an inventory of the few belongings that had been in his pocket. There was a notebook, and he scanned it rapidly. A few pages were missing, and most were blank. There was only a shopping list. That puzzled him for a minute—he couldn't believe he'd taken to using lipstick as well as cigarettes, though both were listed in his handwriting. The notebook contained nothing else.

He stuffed it back into his pockets, along with his keyring. There were more keys than he'd expected, some of which were strange to him, but none held any mark that would identify them. He put a few pennies into another pocket—his entire wealth, now, in a world where no more money would be available to him. He grimaced, dropping a comb into the same pocket.

Then there was only his wallet left. His identification card was there, unchanged. Behind it, where his wife's picture had always been, there was only a folded clipping. He drew it out, hoping for a clew. It was only an announcement of people killed in an airplane crash—and among those found dead was Mrs. Wilbur Hawkes, of New York. It seemed that Irma had never reached Reno for the divorce.

He tried to feel some sorrow at that, but time must have healed whatever hurt there had been, even though he couldn't remember. She had hated him ever since she'd found that he really wasn't willing to please his father by becoming another of the vice-presidents in the old man's bank, with an unearned but fancy salary. He'd preferred teaching mathematics and dabbling with a bit of research into the probable value of the ESP work being done at Duke University. He'd explained why he hated banking; Irma had made it clear that she really needed the mink coat no assistant professor could afford. It had been stalemate—a bitter, seven-year stalemate, until she finally gave up hope and demanded a divorce.

He threw the clipping away, and pulled out the final bit of paper. It was a rent receipt for a cold-water apartment on the poorer section of West End—from the price of eighteen dollars a month, it had to be a cold-water place. He frowned, considering it. Apartment 12. That might explain why his own apartment had been unused, though it made little sense to him. It would probably be watched by now, anyway.

HE jerked to his feet at a sound on the window-sill, but it was only a cat, eyeing the unfinished donut. He threw the food out, and the cat dived after it. Hawkes waited for the touch of ice along his backbone to go away. It didn't.

This time, he tried to ignore it. He picked up the paper and began going through it, looking for something that might give him some slight clew. But there was nothing there. Only a heading on an inside page that stirred his curiosity.

Scientist Seeks Confinement

He glanced at it, noting that a Professor Meinzer, formerly of City College, had appeared at Bellevue, asking to be put away in a padded cell, preferably with a strait-jacket. The Professor had only explained that he considered himself dangerous to society. No other reason was found. Professor Meinzer had been doing private work, believed to relate to his theory that . . .

The panic was back, thick in Hawkes' throat. He jerked back against the wall, his heart racing, while he tried to fight it down. There was no sound from the hall or outside. He forced his eyes back to the paper.

And the paper was surrounded by a golden haze. It burst into a momentary flame as the haze flickered out. Hawkes dropped the ashes from his clammy hands. He hadn't been burned!

You can't escape. Run. They'll get you!

He heard the outside door open, as it had opened a hundred times. But now it could only mean that more were coming. He jerked for the open window.

Something came sailing through the air to hit the sill. Hawkes screamed weakly, far down in his throat, before his eyes could register the fact that it was only the cat again.

Then the cat let out a horrible beginning of a sound, and its poor, half-starved body seemed to turn inside out, with a churning motion that Hawkes could barely see. Blood and gore spattered from it, striking his face and clothes.

He froze, unable to move. Either they were outside in the yard, or whatever frightful weapon they used could work through a closed door. He tried to move, first one way, then the other. His feet remained frozen.

Then steps sounded in the hallway, and he waited no longer. His legs came to sudden life, hurling him over the carcass of the cat and outside. He went charging through the refuse, and then leaped and clawed his way over the fence. The alley was deserted, and he shot down it, to swing right, and into another alley.

It wasn't until his muscles began to fail that he could control himself enough to stop and stumble into a darkened spot among the garbage cans, spent and gasping for breath.

THERE was no sign of anyone following. Hawkes had no idea of how they could trace him—but he was beginning to suspect that nothing was impossible, judging by the results of their weapons. For the moment, though, he seemed to have shaken off pursuit. And the physical fatigue had apparently eased some of his terror.

What had shocked him into losing seven months out of his memory, and still could drive him into absolute terror at the first sign of them?

He couldn't go back to the room, and his own apartment was out of the question. The rain had stopped, mercifully, but he couldn't walk the streets indefinitely, dirty and bedraggled as he was. He tried to think of something to do, but all of his schemes took money which he no longer had.

Finally, he arose wearily. Maybe the apartment for which he had the rent receipt was watched—but he'd have to chance it. There was no place else.

He'd been accidentally heading toward it, and he continued now, sticking to the alleys until he reached West End Avenue. He tried to hurry, but the best his tired muscles could do was a slow shuffle.

Light was beginning to show faintly in the sky, but it was still too early for more than a few cars and a chance pedestrian. At this hour, the avenue was used by only a few cruising cabs, heading toward better sections. He shuffled along, trying to look like a man on his way home after too much night out. The cat blood on his clothes bothered him, until he tried weaving a little as he walked, imitating the drunks he had seen often enough.

He passed an all night diner, and fished for his pennies. But there were several men inside. He went on, past Fifty-ninth Street, heading for the apartment, which should be near Sixty-seventh.

He was just reaching the top of the hill near Sixty-fourth when a gray sedan sped along, heading downtown. There were running boards on it, and behind the wheel sat the slim young man who'd given chase to Hawkes before.

Hawkes tried to duck, but the sedan was already braking and swinging back. It was beside him before he could realize more than the old clamor of his brain, telling him to run, that he couldn't escape.

The car matched his speed, and the driver leaned far to the right. "Will Hawkes," the young man called. "How about a lift?"

The smile was pleasant, and the voice was casual, as if they were old friends. There was no gun in the man's hands. It might have been any honest offer of a ride.

Hawkes braced himself, just as a patrol car turned onto the Avenue ahead. He opened his mouth to scream, but his vocal cords were frozen. The young man followed his eyes to the patrol car, and frowned.

Then the gray sedan lifted smoothly upwards to a height of twenty feet, turned sharply in mid-air, lifted again, and seemed to make a smooth landing on top of a huge garage building!

There had been no roar of jets and no evidence of any means of propulsion.

THE patrol car went on down the Avenue, heading for the diner. The officers inside apparently had missed the whole affair.

Hawkes' cowardly legs suddenly came unfrozen. He was conscious of them churning madly. With an effort, he got partial control of himself, managing to focus on the house numbers.

There were no watchers outside the number he wanted, though they could have been in rooms across the street. He had no choice, now. He leaped up the steps and into the hallway. His eyes darted around, spotting a door that led out to the side, probably into an alley. He drew himself together, hiding behind the stairs.

But there was no further

pursuit for the moment. The fear that seemed to come before each attack was missing. Maybe it meant he was safe for the moment—though it hadn't warned him of the car the young man was driving.

Heat rays! Levitation! Hawkes dropped to his knees as fatigue and reaction caught up with him again, but his mind churned over the new evidence. As a mathematician, he was sure such things could not exist. If they did, there would have been extension of math well in advance of the perfection of the machines, and he'd have known of it as speculative theory, at least. Yet, without such evidence, the devices apparently existed.

The police weren't in on it, that much was certain. It was more than a hunt for a criminal. What had been going on during the months he had missed?

His mind shuttled over the spy-thrillers he had seen. If some nation had the secrets, and he had discovered them . . . But the heat ray would never have been used openly, then; they wouldn't tip their hand. Anyhow, the cold war was still going on, and that would have been pointless when any nation had such power.

And if the secret belonged to the United States, the young man would never have levitated to avoid police at the greater risk of tipping off anyone who saw that such things could be done.

Nothing made sense—not even the crazy feeling of fear that had warned him on some occasions and failed him this last time. The only explanation that was credible was the totally incredible idea that some life, alien to earth and with strange unearthly powers, was after him—or that he was insane.

He fumbled through a pack of cigarettes until he located the last one, streaked with sweat that was still pouring down from his armpit, and lighted it. It was all answerless—just as his sudden need for smoking was.

III

HAWKES crushed out the cigarette and began climbing the wide stairs slowly. It was probably an ambush into which he was heading—but without this place, he had no chance of resting. He stared at the numbers painted on the dirty red doors, and went on up a second flight of stairs. The number he wanted was at the end of the hall, dimly lighted. He dropped to the keyhole, but found it had been filled long ago, probably when the Yale lock was installed.

He put his ear against the door and listened. There was no sound from inside except a monotonous noise that must be water dripping from a leaky faucet. Finally, he climbed to his feet and reached for his keys. The third one he tried fitted, and the door swung open.

He fumbled about, looking for a light switch, and finally struck a match. The switch was a string hanging down from a bare bulb. He pulled it, to find he stood inside one of the old monstrosities with which New York is filled—a combination kitchen and bathroom, with a tiny closet for the toilet in one corner. There was an ice-box, a dirty stove, a Franklin heater connected to the chimney, a small sink, and a rickety table with four folding chairs. In a closet, cheap china showed.

He went through that, into the seven-by-twelve living room. There was a cheap radio, a worn sofa, two more folding chairs and a big typing table. The rug on the floor had been patched together. Then he breathed more easily. Over the back of one of the chairs was a sports jacket which he recognized as his own. He jerked it up suddenly and began going through the pockets, but they had already been emptied.

It didn't matter—he no longer cared why he should be in a place so totally unlike any his usually neat habits would have led him to. It was his.

Then, as he came into the bedroom, he hesitated. It was smaller than the living room, with a bed that took up half of one wall, and two dressers jammed into the remaining space. One corner held a cardboard closet—and hanging on the hook was a man's raincoat and hat, both at least five sizes too big for him. His eyes darted about, to find a strange mixture of things he remembered as his and possessions which he would never have owned. On one of the dressers was a small traveling case, filled with the cosmetics and appliances which only a woman would use.

He jerked open the closet, and his nose told him before his eyes that it held only female clothing! Yet on the shelf, his old hat rested happily.

He could make no sense of it—the place looked as if several people lived in it, and yet it wasn't really fitted for anyone to spend his whole time there. There was none of the accumulation of property that would fit any permanent residence. He went out of the bedroom, passing the typewriter desk. The typewriter was an old, standard Olympia—a German machine he'd refitted with the Dvorak keyboard which he had learned for greater efficiency. He was sure nobody else would want it.

The dishes were dusty, and there was no food in the icebox.

NOW, though, it began to fit—a place where it was convenient to stop in, but not a place to live. And perhaps he had been in the habit of lending it to others. Though why he shouldn't have used his own apartment was something he still couldn't understand.

But it was possible there was no record of this place.

He began shucking off his shirt as he went back through the living room—until the marks on the rug caught his eyes. Something heavy had rested there recently—there had been other desks about, or heavily laden tables. And a bit of paper under the sofa could only have come from one of the complicated computing machines used in high-power mathematics. He scanned the fragment, making no sense of it, except that it was esoteric enough to belong to any new branch of theory. For a second, the heat-rays and levitations entered his head—but none of the symbols fitted such a branch of physical development.

What had been going on here—and why had the machines been removed so recently that their traces still looked fresh?

He shook his head—and froze, as a key turned in the lock.

There was no time for flight. She stood in the doorway, blinking at the light before he could turn. She, of course, was the girl whom he'd barely noticed when he knocked the couple down as he charged out of his apartment.

Of course? He puzzled over that. He'd almost expected it—and yet, now that he looked more closely, he couldn't even be sure that she was the same. She wore the same green jacket, but nothing else he could be sure of, because he had no other memory of that girl. This one was two inches shorter than he was, with dark red hair and the deepest blue eyes he had seen. She looked like an artist's conception of an Irish colleen, except that her mouth was open half an inch, and she was studying him with the look of being about ready to scream.

"Who are you?" He forced the words out at her.

She shook her head, and then smiled doubtfully. "Ellen Ibañez, naturally. You startled me! But you must be Wilbur Hawkes, of course. Didn't you get my wire?"

He watched her, but there had been no stumbling over his name, and no effort to make it sound too casual. Apparently, the name meant nothing to her. He shook his head. "What wire?" Then he plunged ahead, quickly. "You've heard of amnesia? Good. Well, I've got it—partially. If you can tell me anything about myself before yesterday, Miss, I'll never be anything but . . .

He choked on that, unable to finish. And behind the surface emotions, his mind was poised, sniffing for danger. There was no feeling of it, though he kept telling himself alternately that she had been the girl at the door and that she obviously had not been.

He'd seen her before. The tilt of her head, that unmatchable hair . . .

"YOU poor man!" Her voice was all sympathy, and the bag she was carrying dropped to the floor as she came over. "You mean you *really* can't remember—at all?"

"Not for the last seven months!"

She seemed surprised. "But that was when you answered my advertisement. I never saw you—though you did call me, and your voice sounds familiar. You sent me the check, and I mailed you the key. That was all."

"But I must have given you references—told you something—"

Again, she shook her head. "Nothing. You said you were a teacher at CCNY, but that you were quitting, and wanted a place to use as an office. You didn't care what it was like. That's all."

Hawkes felt she was lying—but it could have been true. And in his present state, he probably believed everyone was other than they seemed. He remembered the gray sedan rising to the roof—and the cat turning inside out—

Sickness hit at him. He groped back towards a chair, sinking into it. He'd almost found a refuge, and even hoped that he could find some of the missing past. Now . . .

He must have partially fainted. He heard vague sounds, and then she was putting something against his lips. It was bitter and hot, though it only remotely resembled coffee. He gulped it gratefully, not caring that it was sweet and black. He saw the bottle of old coffee powder, caked with age, and heard the water boiling on the stove. Idly, he wondered whether he'd bought the jar originally or she had. Then his senses snapped back.

"Thanks," he muttered thickly. He groped his way to his feet, his head slowly clearing. "I guess I'd better go now."

She forced him back into the chair. "You're in no condition to leave here, Will Hawkes. Ugh! Your shoes are filthy. Let me help you . . . there, isn't that better? Whatever you've been doing to yourself, you should be ashamed. You're going straight to bed while I clean some of this up!"

His head had sunk back on the table, and everything reached him through a thick fog. It wasn't right—girls didn't act that way to strange men who looked as if they'd come from a Bowery fight. Girls didn't take a man's clothes off. Girls didn't . . .

He let her half carry him into the bedroom, and tried to protest as she put him between clean sheets. He stared at the view of his lavender shorts against the fresh whiteness, while things seemed far away. He'd played with a girl named Ellen, once when he was eleven and she was nine. She'd had bright copper hair, and her name had been—what had it been? Not Ibañez. Bennett, that was it. Ellen Bennett.

He must have said it aloud. She chuckled. "Of course, Will. Though I never thought you'd be the same Will Hawkes. I knew it when I saw that scar on your shoulder, where you cut yourself sliding down our cellar door. Go to sleep."

Sliding down, sliding down into clouds of sleep. Sleep! She'd drugged him! Something in the coffee!

HE jerked up, reaching for her, but she ducked aside, drawing on the tops to a pair of frilly pajamas. "Ellen, you—"

"Shh!" She pulled a robe over the pajamas and lay down, outside the blankets. "Shh, Will. You have to sleep.

You're *so* tired, *so* sleepy . . ."

Her voice was soothing, and the fingers along the base of his neck was relaxing. He reached out a last inquiring finger of doubt for the feeling of danger, and couldn't find it. This was as wrong as the other things had been wrong —but his mind let go, and he was suddenly asleep.

He awoke slowly, with a thick feeling in his mouth. Drugged! And the sense of danger had failed him again! He swung over sharply, reaching for her, but she was gone.

His clothes lay beside him, neatly pressed, and he grabbed for them. There was a pair of socks, too large, but better than none. His muscles felt wrong as he began dressing, but the feeling wore away. The clock said that less than two hours had passed. If she'd put a drug in the coffee, it must have been one to which he was less sensitive than the average. She'd probably never suspected that he would waken.

A trace of fear struck through him, but it was weaker than before, and it seemed normal enough, under the circumstances. He fumbled over the shoelaces, and then grabbed up his coat.

She'd bring *them* back! Maybe they'd used her as a spy!

But he couldn't understand why she'd bothered to press his clothes. And the apartment still puzzled him. Even if her story was true, it simply wasn't the sort of a place where a girl like her would live. Nor was it fixed as she might have arranged a place, even allowing for what he might have done to it in seven months.

He reached automatically for the lock in the dim hall, and realized his hands knew the door, whatever else was true. Then he went out and down the stairs. He heard a babble of kids' voices, part in English and part in a sort of Spanish. That meant that things were normal, to the casual observer along the street. But he knew it was poor evidence that things really were as they should be. He stood in the comparative darkness of the hall, staring out. Nothing was wrong, so far as he could see. He had to risk it.

Hawkes shoved past the women on the steps, and headed down West End, trying not to seem in a hurry. His eyes turned up to the roof of the garage, but he could see nothing there; he'd half-expected that the slim young man would be parked up on the roof, waiting.

THEN the fear began, mounting slowly. He jerked around quickly, scanning the street. For a second, he thought he saw the slim figure, but it was only a back turned to him, and it disappeared into a barber-shop. Probably someone else.

The fear mounted a little, and he found his steps quickening. He cut around the corner, where men were crowded into a little restaurant. He was heading into a dead-end street, but there was an alley leading from it. He had to keep off the main streets.

Footsteps sounded behind him.

He moved faster, and the footsteps also speeded up. He slowed, and they kept on. Then they were nearly behind him, just as he reached the alley and jerked back into it, grabbing for a broken bottle he had spotted.

"Will!" It was a gasping wheeze. "Will! For God's sake, it's only me. I know everything—your amnesia. But let me explain!"

It stopped him. He held the bottle carefully, as the fat figure of an old man stepped softly around the corner, fear written on every aged wrinkle. It was the man he'd stumbled into when he dashed out of his apartment.

But the fear there matched his own so completely that he dropped the bottle. The other man stood trembling, gasping for breath. Then he gathered himself together, though his pudgy hands still clenched tightly, showing white knuckles.

"Will," he repeated. "You must believe me. I know about you. I want to help you—if there's any help for you, God forgive us both. And God have mercy on Earth. It's worse than you can believe—and different. It's . . ."

Horror washed over the old man's face. He stood, fighting within himself. Hawkes felt his own back hairs lift, and he drew back. For a second, the fat man seemed to waver before him, as if his body was only a projection. Then it quieted.

"It—it almost had me for a second."

He turned back to Hawkes, trying to control the quivering muscles in his face. But his victory was still incomplete when he suddenly leaped up.

"Get back, Will. Oh, God, O God!"

He leaped outwards, his fat old legs pumping savagely.

Then the air seemed to quiver.

Where he had been, there was only a dark cloud of smoke, spreading outwards in a rough equivalent of his shape. A spurt of steam leaped upwards savagely, and the smoke seemed darker. It began to drift on the air, touched a building, and left a spot of smudginess, before it drifted on, getting thinner with each gust of wind. It was as if every atom of his body had suddenly disassociated itself from every other atom.

HAWKES found his fingernails cutting his palms, and there was blood flowing from his bitten tongue. He heard a hacking moan in his throat. He struggled against something that seemed to be holding him down, and then leaped at least ten feet, to land running.

The alley was twisted and narrow. He shot down it and around a corner. An ice-house stood there, and he barely avoided the loading trucks. He was back near the apartment building where he'd found the girl, and he doubled to a door that showed. It seemed to be locked, but somehow, he got through it. He seemed to melt through the door, though he wasn't sure whether his lunge smashed it or whether his fingers had found the latch in time.

He ducked around loose-hanging electric wires, under twisted pipes, and across a pile of coal around a hot-water heater. He twisted and turned, to come into complete darkness, and halt short, listening.

The fear was going—and there were again no sounds of pursuit. But he couldn't be sure. He'd heard no sounds when the fat man had leaped out, but they had been there.

Silently and thickly, he cursed. To find a man who seemed to be his friend, and who knew about him—and then to have them kill that man with such horrible efficiency before he could learn what it was all about!

He gagged in the darkness, almost fainting again.

Then, slowly, it was too much. For the moment, he could run no more, and nothing seemed to matter. He understood his sudden bravado no better than the unnatural cowardice that had been riding his shoulders, but he shrugged, and moved forward.

The dark passage led out to steps, that carried him up to the sidewalk, in front of the building. Ellen Ibañez—or Bennett—was less than five feet from him, and her eyes were fixed firmly on his face.

IV

SHE seemed surprised, but tried to smile. "I thought I left you asleep, Will," she said, in a tone that was meant to be bantering. " 'Smatter, the fuse blow?"

He accepted the excuse for his presence in the basement. "Yeah, it did. You left the iron on. I wondered what happened to you?"

"Nothing. Just shopping. There wasn't a bit of food in the place—and I must say, Will, you aren't much of a housekeeper. I bought pounds of soap!"

He followed her up the stairs, and his key opened the door. He was still operating on the general belief that they'd be least likely to spot him where they had already found him once. If the girl had tipped them off, then they had it figured out that he had run off, and probably wouldn't be back.

He hoped so, at any rate.

She was talking too briskly, and she was too careful not to mention that the iron was cool, with its cord wrapped neatly around the handle. He offered no explanation, but let her babble on about the strange coincidence of his being *the* Will Hawkes, and how she'd almost forgotten the childhood days.

"How come the Ibañez?" he asked, finally.

"Stage name! I tried to make a go of the musicals, but it wasn't my line, I found. But the name stuck."

"And where'd you learn how to drug coffee that way?"

She didn't change expression. There was even a touch of a twinkle in her eye. "Waitress in a combination bar and restaurant. You needed the sleep, Will. And I guess I still feel as much of a mother to you as I did when you used to get hurt, so long ago."

She had things out of the bags now, and he saw that she had been doing a lot of shopping. There had still been time enough to call the slim young man, though—or, he suddenly realized, the fat man. He had no more reason to believe her an enemy than a friend. Then he corrected that. If she'd known enough to call the fat man, and had been his friend, she could have told him things. She'd denied knowing anything, though.

He couldn't understand why he trusted her—and yet, somehow, he did. Even if he knew she'd called them, he would still have to trust her. He was sure now that she was lying, and that she had been the girl at the door—but that meant she'd been with the fat man. And the fat man had seemed to be his friend. Or, had the man been set to lure him out, but miscalculated, and gotten only what had been meant for him?

His head was spinning, and he gave it up. He was a fool to trust her simply because the fear feeling subsided around her—but he had nothing better to do than to follow his hunches, and then try to play the odds as best he could.

"CIGARETTES," she said, handing him a pack of his brand. "And for me. Shoe dye—your shoes need it, and I couldn't find a shoe store. I did get a shirt though, and a tie. You'll find a hat in that bag. Size seven and a quarter?"

He nodded gratefully, and went in to change. His old shirt had caught most of the cat's blood, and he needed a fresh one. There were a couple of spots on his trousers, but they'd do. And the sports jacket matched well enough.

He daubed the dye onto his shoes—one of the combined polish and dye things.

"Cold-cuts all right?" she asked, and he called back a vague answer that seemed to satisfy her. He was staring at the shoe dye.

It worked fairly well, when he experimented. He daubed it onto his hair with a wisp of cotton. His hair began to mat down, but he found that combing it out as he went along removed the worst of the wax and still left some of the color. It worked better than it should have done.

He found a bottle of something that smelled of alcohol and belonged in her cosmetics, and began removing most of the mess. By being careful, he got the wax and most of the dye smell off, while leaving his hair darker.

"Better wash up," she called.

There was a razor among the things she had bought. He daubed some of the dye on his upper lip, where the stubble of a mustache was showing. It was easier there, if it didn't wash off in soap and water.

Some of it did, but when he finished shaving, he felt better. It wouldn't pass close inspection, but he now seemed to have darker hair, and the dye had exaggerated the little beginning of a mustache enough to make some change in his appearance.

He waited for her to comment, but she said nothing. He waited for her questions about what he was going to do, and her explanations that of course he couldn't stay there. She merely went on talking idly, while they ate. It didn't fit.

Finally he stood up and began taking down the rope that was strung up over one end of the room, to use as a clothes line, he supposed. She looked up at that. "What—"

"You can fight, if you want to," he told her. "Or you can save yourself the headache of being knocked out. Take your choice. People don't pay much attention to screams in a place like this. And I'm not going to harm you, if you'll take it easily."

"You mean it!" Her eyes were huge in her face, and there was a touch of fright now. She gulped visibly, and then seemed to go limp. "All right, Will. In the bedroom?"

He nodded, and she went ahead of him. She didn't struggle, until he was about to gag her. Then she drew her head aside. "There's money in my bag, if you're going out."

HE swore, hotly and sickly. If she'd only act just once as a normal female should! Maybe Irma had been a hysterical, cold-blooded fool, but she couldn't have been that much different from other women—even the books indicated Ellen should be anything but so damned coöperative!

"If you'll tell me what's going on, I'll still let you go," he suggested, drawing her hands tighter together.

"I can't, Will. I don't know."

He had to believe her—he knew she was telling the truth, at least to some extent. And that made it just so much worse. He bound the gag over her mouth as gently as he could, and closed the door behind him. Her big eyes haunted him as he turned to the telephone.

The information girl at CCNY could only tell him that Wilbur Hawkes had resigned abruptly seven months before, and no one knew where he was—they had heard he was doing government research. He snorted at that—it was always the excuse, when nobody knew anything.

He tried a few other numbers, and gave up. Nobody knew—and nobody seemed to react to his name any differently from what they would have done had he remained a quiet, professorish man, minding his own business, instead of being chased by . . .

He couldn't complete that. The idea was still too fantastic. Even if there were alien life-forms that were subtly invading Earth, why should they pick on him? What good could a little, unimportant mathematician do them—particularly if they had the powers he already knew they possessed? It was a poor answer, though no harder to believe than that any group on Earth could so suddenly come up with miracles.

Anyhow, men knew enough already to be pretty sure that Mars and Venus wouldn't have creatures that could invade Earth—and the other planets were hopeless. Perhaps from another star—but that would mean violating the theories of mass-increase with the speed of light, and he was not ready to accept that, yet.

This time, he went out of the building without looking first. It could do no good—they could hide from him, he knew, and he would only call attention to himself by looking around. With the change in appearance, he might get by. He moved rapidly up to Broadway, where he found a little clothing store and a ready-made suit that nearly fitted him. The tailor there seemed unconcerned when he insisted the cuffs be turned up at once, and that he wanted to wear it immediately. It took nearly an hour, but he felt safe, for a change. A five-and-ten furnished a pair of heavy-rimmed glasses that seemed to have blanks in them, and he decided he might get by.

There was no evidence of pursuit. He caught a cab, and headed for the library. Ellen had been well-heeled—suspiciously so for a girl who lived in a cold-water flat like that; he'd peeled fifteen tens from her wallet, and there'd been more, not to mention the twenties. His conscience bothered him a bit, but he was in no position to worry too much.

THE library was still the puzzle of the ages to him—he'd used it half his life, and still found it impossible to guess why such a building had been chosen. But eventually, he found the periodical room, and managed to get through the red tape enough to be given a small table with a stack of newspapers and magazines.

The mathematics magazines interested him most. He pored through them, looking for a single hint of the things he had seen. Einstein's work with gravity stood out, but no real advances had come from it. It was still a philosophical rather than an actual attack on physics—as beautiful as a new theology, and about as hard to utilize. He skimmed through the pages, but nothing showed. No real advance had been made since his memory blanked out, except for one paper on variable stars which was interesting, but unhelpful.

He threw them aside in disgust. He knew that it was useless to look in other languages. Work couldn't be done without some first stages that would be reported, and any significant new theory would be picked up and spread. Science wasn't yet completely under political wraps.

For a second, he stopped as he came to a paper bearing his by-line. Then he grimaced—it was an old one, just published—his attempt to find how the phenomena of poltergeists could be fitted into the conservation of energy, and his final proof that the whole business was sheer rubbish. It would be nice to be able to get back to a life where he could fool around with such learned jokes.

The newspapers, beginning with the last day he could remember, were almost as barren of results. There was the story of the cold war, without the strange overtones that should be there if any of the major powers—where all the major scientists would tend to be—had found something new. He'd studied the statistical analysis of mob psychology at times, and felt sure he could spot the signs.

He skimmed on, without results, until he finally came to the current paper. This he read more carefully. There was no mention of him. But he found something on the fat man. It was a simple follow-up to the story about the scientist who'd turned himself in at Bellevue—the man had mysteriously disappeared, three hours later. And there was a picture—the face of the fat man, with "Professor Arthur Meinzer" under it.

It didn't help.

Hawkes shoved the magazines and papers back, and went through the series of halls and stairs that led him to the main reference room, inconveniently located on the top floor. He found the book he wanted, and thumbed rapidly through it. Meinzer was listed on the bottom of page 972—but as he looked for 973, a pile of ashes dribbled onto the floor.

There was no use. They'd gotten there ahead of him.

He made one final attempt. He called the college, asking for Meinzer, to find that nobody even knew the name! He knew they were lying—but he could do nothing about that. Maybe it was only because of the publicity—or maybe because someone or something had gotten to them first!

FEAR was growing with him as he came out on the street. He ducked into a crowd, and headed slowly into a corner drug store, trying to seem inconspicuous, but the fear mounted. They were near—they would get him! Run, GO!

He fought it down, and found that it was weakened, either by his becoming used to it or because the urgency was less than it had been.

He ducked into a phone-booth and called the newspaper, keeping his eye on both entrances to the store. It seemed to take forever to locate the proper man there, but finally he had his connection.

"Meinzer," the voice said, with a curious doubtfulness.

"Oh, yeah. Mister, that story's dead! Call up . . ."

The telephone melted slowly, dropping into a little cold puddle on the floor!

Hawkes had felt the tension mounting, and he was prepared for anything. Now he found himself on the street, darting across Forty-second Street against the light, without even remembering having left the booth. He stole a quick glance back, to see people staring at him with open mouths. He thought he saw a slim figure in gray tweeds, but he couldn't be sure—and there were probably thousands of such men in New York.

He ducked into a bank, wormed his way around the various aisles, and out the back entrance. A cab was waiting there, and he held out a bill.

"I'm late, buddy. Penn Station!"

The cab-driver took the bill and the hint, and darted out, just as the light was changing.

Penn Station was as good a place to try to get lost from pursuit as any. Hawkes examined his wallet, considering trying to get a train out—but he'd used up nearly all he had taken from Ellen.

And all his careful disguise had proved useless. They weren't fooled—and this business of dodging was wearing thin. By now, they'd know his habits!

He drew out a coin, flipping it. It came up heads. He frowned, but there was nothing else to do. He moved down the ramp toward the subway that would carry him back to Sixty-sixth and Broadway. He was probably walking into their trap by now, but the coin was right. He had to free Ellen. If they got him, it couldn't be much worse for him.

Then he shuddered. He couldn't know whether it would be worse for his country, or even his world. He couldn't really know anything.

V

IT was growing dark as he walked down Sixty-sixth, eyeing every man suspiciously, and knowing his suspicion would do no good. He was still trying to think, though he knew his thoughts were as useless as his suspicions.

If he could remember! His mind came up sharply against leaving Irma and taking out the mail; then it went abruptly blank. What had been in the letter? It had been from a professor—it might have been from Professor Meinzer. That would tie in neatly. But Meinzer was dead, and he couldn't remember. They'd stripped him of his memory. How? Why? Were they trying to prevent his giving information to others—or were they trying to get something from him? And what could he know?

He'd dabbled with ESP mathematically, but now he found himself wondering if it could exist. Could they be tracking him by some natural or mechanical ability to read his mind? He strained his own mind to find a whisper of foreign thought, outside his brain. He drew a blank, of course, as he'd expected.

There were no answers. They could play with him, like a cat juggling a mouse, letting him almost learn something—and then, always, they arrived just in time to prevent his success!

Put a rat in a maze where it can't learn the path, and it goes insane. But what good would he be to anyone if they drove him insane? And why bother with all that when they could silence him as well by killing him?

He'd forgotten to watch, and was surprised to find his feet on the steps of the apartment building. He jerked back, and bumped into someone.

"Sorry." The words came from behind him, automatically, and he turned to see the slim young man stepping aside. For a second, their eyes met squarely. A row of teeth flashed in a brief smile as the man started around him. "Guess I was thinking. Should have watched where I was going."

The man went on down the street, and turned in at the restaurant entrance.

HAWKES lifted a foot that weighed a ton and slowly closed his mouth. He'd been facing away from the street light—and his face might have been hard to see. Yet . . .

It didn't fit. The young man must have known him!

He blanked it from his mind. He couldn't believe that it was anything but lack of recognition. It was hard to see here, where the other was facing the light, and he was in the shadow.

But it still meant that they were waiting, nearby.

He dashed up the stairs, expecting a rush at both landings. The normal sounds of the apartment house went on. He listened at his door, but he could hear nothing except the same drip he had heard before. Slowly, he inserted the key and went in. The small bulb was still on. He crept along, trying to move silently on floors that insisted on creaking. The living room was as he had left it, and he caught sight of Ellen on the bed.

He spotted a mirror over one of the dressers, and used that to study more of the bedroom. It seemed as empty as before.

Finally, he stepped inside. There was no one there but Ellen, and she seemed to be asleep, doubled up in a position that might have made the unkind cords easier to stand. She moaned slightly as he untied her gently, but didn't awaken. Her breathing was regular, and her breath had the odd muskiness of someone who has slept for several hours.

He found a bottle of liquor on the shelf where she had put it, and rinsed out a couple of glasses. It was good liquor —good enough to take without mixers, as they'd have to do.

She came awake when he called her, rubbing her eyes and then her wrists, where the cords had left a mark. But she was smiling. "Hi, Will. I knew you'd come back. Hey, not on an empty stomach."

"You need it—and so do I," he told her. "Bottoms up!"

They were big glasses. She gasped over it, but she downed it, then reached for the water he had brought as a chaser. She swallowed, and blinked tears out of her eyes. "I don't usually drink."

He made no comment, but refilled the glass. The liquor had less effect on him than he'd expected, though he'd always had a good head for it. It took some of the edge off his worrying, though.

She giggled suddenly, and he frowned. She couldn't take much on an empty stomach, it seemed. Then he shrugged. Let her drink—maybe if he could get her drunk, he could find something out; at least he might learn whether the slim young man had been there during the day.

"Like when you found your dad's cider," she said, and giggled again. "You got awful —hp!—awful drunk, Willy, din't you? You were — so — funny!"

She was trying to be careful with her words already. She slid around, doing things that brought more honestly beautiful thigh into the light than Will had seen in ten years. He reached to adjust her dress, and she giggled again, sliding against him.

"You kissed me then, Willy. Remember? Bet you don' remember!"

HE began it coldly, deliberately. If he could work on her emotions enough, he'd crack the wall of evasion and lies, somehow. He reached for her, calculating what would arouse her without causing any shock to bring her back to her senses.

He hadn't counted on the quickness of her reponse, nor the complete acceptance of his right with which she took it. The liquor had reduced her to the stage of a little girl who competely trusted her companion. She seemed as unconscious of her body as a child might be.

Instead of protesting, she reached down and began unfastening the buttons on her dress. " 'Syour turn now, Willy. Put you to bed last night, you put me to bed t'-night. Then you gotta kiss me good-night. Nighty-night, nighty-night."

He felt like a heel at first. And then he began to feel like a man—any man around a beautiful girl half-undressed, and getting more so.

She slipped under the sheets, tossing out the last of her clothing, and crooning happily. "Gotta kiss me good-night, Willy. Nighty-night!"

He yanked the pull-cord savagely, cutting off the light, and fumbling in the darkness. After what seemed hours of awkwardness, he slid in beside her, feeling her arms go around him in complete acceptance. To hell with *them!* They could chase him some other time!

He pulled her to him, while his blood beat in his neck, and he began to lose any conscious volition of what he was doing. He drew her tighter, while a great clot of emotion set fire to his brain. He—

Cold beyond anything he had known bit at him. A tremendous pressure within him seemed about to force him to explode outwards, and the shock jerked him into full awareness.

In a split second, he swung his eyes from the great, jagged landscape on which he stood, up an impossible range of mountains that were all harsh blacks and cold whites, to a cold black sky in which the stars were blazing specks without a flicker. He saw the Earth above him, bigger than the moon had ever been, and with the dim outlines of continents showing through the soft stuff that must be clouds.

He was on the moon! And naked, without air!

ALMOST at once, something clapped down around him, and the pressure let up, while heat seemed to leap into the rocks under his feet and make them comfortable. He gulped down the air that somehow seemed to stay close to him, instead of evaporating into the vacuum.

The moon! Now they had him!

Fear blazed in him — a stark, unreasoning terror that was like a physical thing. *Run —but you can't run! They've got you! You can't escape!*

The light blotted out, and then snapped on, more strongly. He stood in the kitchen of the cold-water apartment, still naked, with bits of chalky dust between his toes.

He had no time for reason. His brain seemed to have jumped over a hurdle and come down in a puddle beyond, foul with the stuff it had found there. He heard Ellen shriek, and then cry out again.

He lurched into the bedroom, while she let out another gurgling cry as the light showed him in the doorway. She came out of the bed, leaping for him, crying his name —cold sober! But he wanted none of her act. He shook her off.

"You damned alien! You filthy monster, disguised as a girl! When you get in a spot where I'm sure to find you out, you have a cute trick up your sleeve — but it won't work. You can send me back there—back to the rest of your kind, from wherever they came. But you won't fool me into thinking you're human again. You can't pass one test!"

He wouldn't be fooled into thinking it was a dream, either. He'd been physically on the moon—the very dust on his feet proved that. They might drive him insane, but they wouldn't do it that way.

She was crying now, gasping out words that he only half heard. "I'm human, Will. Oh, I'm human!"

"Then prove it! Come here, and prove it!"

She cried again at that, as he pulled her down with him. But slowly her crying quieted.

He awoke slowly, with sunlight streaming in the windows, and reached for her. He owed her more apologies than one, though he wasn't too sorry about most of it. She had proven herself human. And virginally so. Her complete surrender still left something warm inside him, where only the madness and the fear had been before.

Then he jerked upright, as he found her gone. He cursed himself for a fool, and listened for a stir and bustle from the kitchen, but there was none.

HE was getting used to dressing with a feeling of dire pressure driving him on. He finished rapidly, and yanked the bedroom door open, just as he heard the outer lock click. She was coming in with a bottle of cream and a package of sausage as he reached the kitchen, and there was a smile tucked into the corner of her mouth.

And this time, he knew she wouldn't have betrayed him. Yet the fear increased in him. He darted past her as she leaned to kiss him, heading for the door. The room seemed to quiver. The hall was filled with a faint golden haze!

He had to get out! He jerked backwards, caught her hand, and pulled her. "Ellen! We've got to get out!"

It was a half-articulate shout, and she resisted, but he began dragging her after him. Something fumbled at the lock, and a key slipped into it. The door opened.

Hawkes didn't know what kind of an alien he expected. He knew that men could never have thrown him to the moon and back, not in another thousand years. It had to be a monster.

But he should have known that monsters here came in human form—they'd have to.

The fear rose to a shriek in his brain, and then died down as the human form entered. It was too normal—too familiar. A medium-sized man, dressed in a suit as inconspicuous as his own, wearing a silly little mustache that no outland monster should ever wear.

The creature jumped in, slamming the door behind it. "Stay there! You can't risk it outside now! We've got to—"

Hawkes hit the figure with his shoulder, in the best football fashion he could muster. It could try—but it couldn't keep him and Ellen here to be burned in their heat-ray bath, or treated to whatever alien torture they had in mind. He felt his shoulder hit. And he knew he'd missed. It was an arm that he struck against, and the arm brought him upright, while a second arm drew back and came forward with a savage right to his jaw.

He went out with a dull plopping sound in his brain. Then, slowly, an ache came out of the blackness, and the beginning of sound. He was fighting out of the unconsciousness, fighting against time and the monster who'd try to steal Ellen.

But Ellen's hands were on his head, and an ice-cold towel was wet against his forehead. "Will! Will!"

HE groaned and sat up. The other—alien or human—was gone.

"Where—?" he began.

She was trying to help him to his feet, and he got up groggily, with his head beginning to clear.

"He just ran out, Will." Ellen was crying, this time almost silently, with the words coming out between shakes of her shoulders. "Will, we've got to get out. We've got to. The men are coming for you. They'll be here any minute. And it's wrong—it won't work! Oh, Will, hurry!"

"Men? Men are coming?" He'd almost forgotten that it could be men who were after him.

"I called them, Will. I thought I had to. But it won't work. Will, do anything you like, but *get* out! They are fools. They . . ."

He opened the door and peered out the doorway into the hall, which seemed quiet. He'd been a fool again. He'd trusted her for some reason, as if a body and loyalty had to go together. They'd been smart, picking a virgin for the job. It must have cost them plenty, unless they'd twisted her mind somehow. Maybe they could do it.

But he knew that whatever they looked like, it couldn't be real men who'd meet him out there.

"Why?" he asked, and was surprised at the flatness of his voice.

She shook her head. "Because I'm a fool, Will. Because I thought they could help you—until *he* came! And because I'm still in love with you, even if you'd forgotten me."

But the fear inside him was drowning out her words, and the golden haze was faint in the air again.

"Okay," he said finally. "Okay, don't burn her, too, now that she's done your dirty work. I'm coming."

The haze disappeared slowly, and he started down the stairs, still holding her hand.

VI

THERE were men with guns in the street. He'd heard two shots as he came down the stairs, and had shoved Ellen behind him. But it was silent now. People with dazed, frightened faces were still darting into the houses, leaving the street to the men with the guns.

Hawkes marched forward grimly, perversely stripped of fear, even though he was sure some of the men out there were monsters and others were their dupes. He tapped one of the men on the shoulder.

"Okay, here I am. The girl goes free!"

The man spun around as if mounted on a ball bearing and pulled by strings. The gun fell from his hands. His emotion-taut face loosened suddenly, seemed to run like melted wax, and congealed again in an expression of utter idiocy. He gargled frothily, and then screamed—high and shrill, like a tortured woman.

Suddenly he was a lunging maniac, tearing up the street.

Now the others were running—some toward cars, and some toward the corners, running flat and desperately on the flat of their feet, without any spring to their motions.

Hawkes jerked his eyes down toward the big gas-storage tanks where most of them had been, and the glow that had been in the corner of his vision was gone. Men seemed to be coming out of a trance. They were breaking away, forgetting about their guns and fleeing.

Three men alone were left.

Hawkes ducked back into the hall of the apartment, dragging Ellen with him. The glass of the door was somewhat dirty, but it made a dim mirror. He could see the slim young man and two others still there. The two men darted into a waiting car, and the leader turned up the street, running smoothly toward the apartment house.

Hawkes could make no sense of it—unless it was another of the seeming tricks designed to drive him out of his mind. He had decided he was one of the rats in the maze that didn't go crazy—the pressure could drive him somewhat mad, but it couldn't keep him that way.

He didn't wait to see what had happened, or whether the sirens that were sounding now were reinforcements for the men with guns or the police. He didn't bother with the slim young man any more. They'd apparently used their dupes to frighten out the people, and then had scared off the dupes—the poor humans who didn't know what it was all about. Now two of the three were gone, and the third monster was coming for him.

He'd escaped before. But sooner or later, they'd catch him—once they were sure he wouldn't be driven insane.

Or was this the beginning of insanity—a delusion of power, a feeling that he could escape? He could never know, if it was. He had to assume that he was sane.

HE CROUCHED back behind the stairs, while the young man in the gray tweeds dashed up them. Then he headed out into the street. The siren was near now—and tardily, he realized that the siren might herald the coming of the real monsters. It was as easy to look like a cop as any other human!

He jerked open the door of the nearest car, pulled Ellen in, and kicked the motor to life. He gunned away from the curb, tossed it into second, and twisted around the corner, straight toward the siren that was nearest. At the last minute, he jerked to the side of the street, to let the police car shoot by. "Never run from a tiger—run toward it. It sometimes works, and it's no worse."

The car was a big one, and the motor purred smoothly. He glanced down at the dash, and frowned. There was no key in the switch. For a second, he stared at it, and then grinned. He'd picked a monster's car, apparently—they'd done a neat job of duplicating, but they didn't need all the safeguards that humans used, and the switch had obviously been a dummy.

He looked at the buttons on the dash, wondering which would make it levitate. But he had no desire to test it, nor to stay in an auto which could probably be traced so easily.

He braked to a halt outside the subway and led Ellen down.

"We're down to the last hole," he told her as the train pulled out of the station. "How much money do you have?"

She shook her head, and held up her arm. "I left it, Will."

They were beyond the last hole, then. He realized now that as long as they'd been in a crowded apartment house, filled with other humans, it had proved a tough nut to crack for the aliens. But on the move . . .

"Maybe we have a chance," he told her. "If humans were after me, it'd be tough—but these things have to avoid the police."

She looked at him, misery on her face. "There are no aliens, Will. Those men you saw were F. B. I. men. That's where I reported you."

"You . . ."

He stared at her, but she was serious.

"But there was nothing about me in the papers, Ellen."

She pointed across the aisle. Spread over two columns on the front page, an older picture of him showed plainly. And even at the distance, the heading was boldly legible.

$100,000 REWARD FOR THIS MAN!

He stared at the figure twice, unbelieving. He was no longer alone against a small group of humans or aliens. Now every living human on the face of the planet would be looking for him!

HE COULD feel their hot breath on his neck, feel eyes staring at him through the papers. Fear began to rise in him, to be halted as the train ground to a new station. Ellen jerked him out, and he moved with her. It wasn't safe to be too long with one group, until they began to wonder and compare faces!

"But what—"

She shook her head. "Nothing, Will. I don't know. What can we do?"

He'd been wondering, while they moved quietly through the groups of people, and up the stairs. There was no place left. He had about a dollar in change, and that would be of no use to them. They'd have to dig a hole in the ground and pull it over them . . .

It joggled his memory, and he grabbed her hand and jerked open the door of a cab that was waiting for the light. He barked out an address—— the corner of Tenth Avenue and one of the streets below Twentieth. The driver got into motion, not bothering to look back. The address was near enough to where Hawkes wanted to be—an old warehouse, with a loading platform. He'd played there as a kid, climbing back under it and digging holes down into the damp, soft earth, as kids have always done. He'd been by there since, and it had remained unchanged.

Sooner or later, the aliens would locate them. But it would give Ellen and him a chance to rest—perhaps long enough for him to waylay someone at night and steal enough for them to leave town. That wouldn't be much help—but it was all he had left to count on.

He saw trucks loading there, as he paid the cab-driver. His heart sank abruptly, until he studied the way the big trailer was parked. If he watched carefully, he could slip under it from the side, and there was a chance he wouldn't be seen.

He darted beneath it.

Luck, for once was with him as he drew Ellen under the trailer and the platform. The old opening was covered with rubble, but he scraped it aside, and found an entrance barely big enough for them to wiggle through. Then they were back in a dark pocket under the back of the platform, barely big enough for them to sit upright. The hole had seemed bigger when he was a kid.

Outside, he heard a boy's voice yelling. "Monster attacks cops! Monster kills five cops! Extra Paper!"

Now he was a monster, to be shot on sight, probably.

"I shouldn't have brought you into this, Ellen," he said bitterly. "I should have left you. You don't even know what's going on—you haven't the faintest idea. If it were just humans, as you think . . ."

She snuggled against him in the coldness of the little cave. "Shh. I got you into it. I—I ratted on you, Scarface!"

BUT he couldn't reply to her attempt at humor. There was no fear now—not even the relief of fear. He'd felt brave for a few minutes, back in the hallway of the apartment. Now the chips were down, and sunk. They were here, in a dank hole, without food, and without a chance, while all the world searched for him to kill him—and while still-unknown aliens with unknown reasons played out their little game with consummate skill that would inevitably locate him.

It might take them a day—they probably would do nothing to him until night came, and the warehouse street was deserted! Ten more hours!

If he only knew what they wanted of him, or why! If he could remember!

He sat there, numbed within himself. Ellen leaned her head forward onto his lap, and he began stroking her hair softly. He'd have liked to have had a chance with her. One night wasn't enough for a whole life. He reached down to draw her face to his . . .

Fear hit him, as something rustled behind him. He tried to turn and look, but his neck refused. The fear grew to panic, and swelled higher as the golden haze began to spread over the little cave. Then his muscles snapped his head around sharply. The slim young man was crawling toward them, holding something that looked like a flashlight. Behind it, he could see the tense lips drawn back over clenched teeth. The man wasn't smiling now. He opened his mouth, just as the thing like a flashlight sprang into light.

No time seemed to elapse, but suddenly Ellen and the young man were both gone, and he sat in the dark hole, alone. He let out an animal cry, and dashed out, crawling through the opening, and kicking the rubble back as he went. He slipped out, and under the trailer. But there was no sign. They'd taken her, and left him unconscious!

He groaned, trying to figure. He'd always gone back to the same place to hide, since he'd found it. They must expect him back there. They'd take Ellen there and wait for him, drugging her, changing her mind, setting her up to use against him. The first time hadn't worked, but they'd try it again. It had to be that. If they hadn't taken her there, he had no way of finding her, and he had to find her.

He began running down the street, forcing himself to believe she was there. Then he slowed. It would do no good to have them all notice him, here on the street. Someone might recognize him then. He turned around, walking back to the bus stop. There were still two dimes and a nickel in his pocket.

HE HUNCHED down on the seat of the bus that seemed to crawl up Tenth Avenue. But no one noticed him in the almost empty vehicle. He got off at Sixty-Sixth and forced himself to walk to West End, up that to the apartment-house.

Men were drawing up in cars—men with guns in their hands. He made a final dash for the apartment entrance. This must be the real show—for which the other had been only a dress rehearsal to throw him off balance. They could wait.

He fumbled with the lock, until he finally got it open. Then he jumped in, slamming the door shut behind him. Ellen stood there, and the creature that had assaulted him before was pawing at her. But he had no time for the monster.

"Stay there!" he shouted at her. "You can't risk it outside now! We've got to—"

He saw she wasn't listening to him. He had to get rid of the creature somehow, if he could get it far enough away from her. Then they'd find someway to get outside, without going out through the entrance.

The creature sprang at him awkwardly. His arm darted down to catch one shoulder, and his right hand swung back and up. There was a savage satisfaction in seeing the creature crumple.

Ellen's voice reached him. "Will! Will, before I go crazy . . ."

"You're free," he told her. "Go down the fire escape and leave that here. I'll get rid of them out front somehow."

He shut the door again, and went down. The words had sounded brave enough, but there had been no courage behind them. Fear still rode him, like the little golden haze that again hovered over him, showing they had spotted him.

He walked out, with it thick around him, rising slowly in temperature. They had him—but Ellen might get away. He walked down the steps, his hands up. They drew back, surprise and something else on their features, their eyes on the haze that surrounded him. They were shouting, but he couldn't hear the words over the shrieks of the people along the street, rushing inside or trying to drag their kids to safety.

Hawkes doubled his legs under him and leaped. He was still attacking the tiger—the slim young man, down by the big gas-storage tanks, directing the new crop of human dupes.

His charge carried him there, while the young man slipped aside. Then someone fired a gun.

He heard the young man yell hoarsely. "No shooting! Stop it! Damn it, NO SHOOTING!"

They weren't paying any attention to the shouts. Bullets ticked against the tanks. Hawkes ducked frantically, physical fear knotting his stomach.

SUDDENLY, he seemed to jerk upwards, to find himself suspended in mid-air, fifty feet off the ground, just beyond the tanks. He stared down at the men, dizzy with the height, but no longer surprised by anything. The men were pointing their guns upwards, while the young man leaped about among them. Bullets were splatting out, though none came near Hawkes. They semed to rico-

chet off the air a few feet in front of him.

The slim young man drew back. And now, the rubble and stones along the street began to lift, and to drive savagely at the attackers. A gale swept along the street, though Hawkes could feel no breath of air, and the force of it was enough to knock most of them down.

They got up and began running, dashing away from the super-science that the young man now seemed bent on turning against his own troop of dupes, now that they were out of control.

Hawkes came drifting downward. He started to cry out in fear, until he noticed that the ground was coming up at him slowly, and that he was slipping sideways. He landed on a street back of the tanks, as gently as a feather.

Surprisingly, everyone was gone when he risked a glance back at the scene of the fight, with the back of the slim man just darting into the apartment house. Then Hawkes cursed, as the creature came darting out, with Ellen behind him, to leap into a car and drive off. The sound of sirens grew louder, and a police car swung onto West End.

Hawkes straightened up slowly, as it hit him. It had

been the same scene he'd gone through before that morning—but with himself in the middle! He shot a glance at the sun, to see it still to the east, though his memory of the day indicated it should have been after noon.

Time! They'd twisted him back through time—the weapon that had looked like a flashlight must have tossed him hours backwards, instead of knocking him out. He'd been attacking himself there in the hallway of his apartment! He'd knocked himself out. And the fight he had just been through was the same fight that he had seen come to its end before!

Now, his younger self and Ellen must be just fleeing toward the hideout under the loading platform, with the slim man still following. If he could get there in time, before the man could run off with Ellen. . . .

VII

THE paper he'd found kept the other passengers on the bus from seeing him, but he was too deep in his own thoughts to read it. His eyes roamed back to the story of the cop-killing monster—a seemingly harmless florist in Brooklyn who'd suddenly gone berserk and rushed down the streets with a knife; he'd been wrong in thinking that concerned him. And he'd been wrong in thinking anyone would try to kill him on sight. The reward notice and picture were in front of his eyes—but it was a reward for information, and there was a huge box that proclaimed he was *not* a criminal and must not be harmed, or even allowed to know he was recognized.

The new facts only confused the issue. He twisted about in his mind, trying to explain why the young man had left him to drift down, and gone rushing into the apartment. He was ready for the collecting—and he'd been left uncollected!

The girl had said there were no aliens. Now he wondered. She had known more than he'd found from her—she'd known his brand of cigarettes, even. And there had been that shopping list, with the lipstick on it—the same type he now remembered her using. He'd known her before—and not just as a little girl. That tied him in with Meinzer, who was a mystery in himself.

He puzzled over it. The things that had happened to him had always been preceded by violent emotion, instead of followed by it. Usually, it had been fear—but sometimes some other emotion, as had been the case just before he was suddenly shifted to the Moon. Whenever he seemed on the verge of discovering something or emotionally upset, it hit at him. Did that mean he was only susceptible to the phenomena when off balance? It still didn't account for the fact that some of the things hadn't directly affected him, at all.

The more he knew, the less he knew.

He got off the bus and headed for the warehouse. This time, he had to wait before he could see a chance to dart under the trailer and into the entrance. He noticed that the gray sedan was parked nearby.

He darted in.

They were still there! He heard Ellen's voice, sounding as if she had been crying, and then an answer from the other. He felt his way carefully over the rubble, working as close as he could. Now, if he sprang the few feet . . .

". . . must be a time-jump," the man's voice said, doubtfully. "I tell you, Ellen, those damned fools were firing at him, up there in the air, while you were still with him in the apartment. That's an angle on this psi factor stuff we hadn't expected."

The voice stopped for a moment. Then it picked up again. "Drat it! I wish you hadn't called the F. B. I. on him—they got rattled when he came out looking like a saint in a halo and jumped fifty feet up to float around. Some fool started shooting, and the rest joined in."

"I had to—he was talking about alien monsters. I thought he was going crazy, Dan. I couldn't tell him anything—I promised him I wouldn't, and I kept my promise. But I thought enough of them might catch him, somehow . . . Dan, can't we find him now? He needs us!"

HAWKES lay frozen. He tried to move forward, but his body was tensed, waiting for more. If something happened now . . .

"Alien monsters?" Dan's voice grew bitter. "It is alien—and a monster. This psi factor . . ."

The words blurred, and seemed to echo and re-echo inside Hawkes' head. That made twice he'd heard them mention the psi factor—the strange ability a few human minds had to perform seeming miracles. Men who had it could make dice roll the way they wanted. Young girls sometimes had it before puberty, and could throw heavy objects around a room without touching them; they did not even know they were the cause of the motion, but blamed it on poltergeists. Other men caused strange accidents—fires, for instance—the old salamander legend!

There'd been a piece of paper—psi equals alpha, the psi factor was the beginning of infinity for mankind. But it had been wrong. He'd changed that, on the other side. It should have read psi equals omega, the absolute end.

He gasped hoarsely, and heard their startled voices stop, while the flashlight beam swung around, to pick him out in the darkness. He felt Ellen and her younger brother, Dan, pulling him forward into the little cave with them, and he heard their voices questioning him. But his head was spinning madly under the sudden flood of memories that the missing key word had suddenly brought back.

The letter from Professor Meinzer had been about his paper on poltergeists which the old man had seen before publication. He'd been doing research on the psi factor for the government, and he needed a mathematician—even one who proved something which he knew wasn't true, provided the mathematics could handle his theories.

Hawkes' head was suddenly brimming with mental images of the seven months, while he worked on the mathematics to tie down the strange pattern of brain waves the old professor had found in the minds of those who had the mysterious psi factor. Dan had worked with them, in the little cluttered apartment, building the apparatus they needed. It was through Dan that Ellen was hired, as a general assistant and secretary.

There had been only the four of them, working in deepest secrecy in the three rooms which the government had felt were more suitable to maintain complete security than any deeply buried laboratory could have been. Ellen made a pretense of living there, and it was a neighborhood where no landlady worried about the men who went to a girl's place, provided everything was quiet.

They'd succeeded, too—they had found the tiny bundle of cells that controlled the psi factor, and learned to stimulate them by artificial wave trains and hypnosis. But the small group in the top division of the government to whom they were responsible had demanded more proof.

HAWKES had treated himself secretly, not knowing that Meinzer had done the same two days before. And both had learned the same thing. The wild talents appeared, but they couldn't be controlled. Meinzer hadn't found security in the hospital, hard as he'd tried to find it. He'd gotten up in the middle of the night and walked through the solid wall, unable to stop until he was back with the group.

Hawkes had tried another way to stop the wild abilities that operated without his conscious control. He'd prepared a new hypnotic tape, worded to make him forget everything he knew, or even the fact that he had worked on the psi factor. He'd put in commands that would make him avoid any reference to it, so that he couldn't learn accidentally. He'd ordered his brain to have nothing to do with it. Then he'd drugged himself with a combination of opiates and hypnotics that should have knocked out a horse. Then he'd telephoned Dan to have men pick him up in an hour and keep him drugged. He'd turned on the tape recorder and stumbled back to the bed.

He groaned, as he remembered his failure. "It's the ultimate, absolute alien, all right—the back of a man's own mind. It's Freud's unconsciousness, or id. The psi factor is controlled by that, and not by the conscious mind. And the id is a primitive beast —it operates on raw impulse, without reason or social consciousness. Every man's unconsciousness is back in the jungle, before civilization—and we've given that alien thing the greatest power that could exist when we wake up the psi power."

"Meinzer thought it was controlled, for a while," Ellen said. "He came when Dan and I called him. I went with him up to your apartment, while Dan got the men to carry you away. But we couldn't reach you—Meinzer barely touched the tape-recorder when something seemed to pick us up and drive us out of the room and down the stairs. We were just going back when you came out."

She shuddered, and Hawkes nodded. He'd obviously used that psi factor to throw off the drugs at the first sign of anyone near him. He told them sickly what had happened to the old man.

"So I killed him," he finished bitterly.

Dan shook his head. "No. Your psi factor works differently. You control heat and radiation, you can move yourself or any object in space for almost any distance, instantly if you want, and it seems you can do the same through time. But you can't disintegrate things, as Meinzer could. He had a suicide urge—we knew that before. When it got out of control again, he blew himself up—just as your dominant urge to protect yourself did all those things around you."

HAWKES grimaced. It wasn't pleasant to know that he'd been doing all the things he'd blamed on monsters. He'd somehow remembered that someone was supposed to come to get him, and he'd run out in wild fear, while his unconscious mind blasted the apartment with heat to destroy all traces. He'd blasted down the subway entrance with another bolt of energy to make his getaway. The poor cat had surprised him, and been killed. His unconsciousness gone wild had tossed Dan's car two hundred feet to the roof of the garage. When it found him losing control emotionally with Ellen, it hadn't let his conscious brain give it the information it needed—it had simply thrown him completely off Earth, pulled air to him, and warmed the rocks. Then, when it found the Moon unfit for life, it had thrown him back to his own world. It had tossed him hours back in time this morning, and lifted him into the air while it pelted his "enemies" with rocks, and built a wall around him by throwing the bullets back instantly.

And it had somehow clung to the implanted idea that he must not find out about himself. It had destroyed anything where the written word might give him a hint, and had even melted the telephone so that he couldn't continue listening to other evidence.

It had probably done a thousand other things that he couldn't even remember, whenever its wild, reasonless fears were aroused and it decided that he had to be protected!

"You should have killed me," he told them. But he knew that they couldn't have done it.

"We had to let you sweat it out. You made us promise not to tell you anything, and we thought you might be right," Ellen told him. "We thought that it might adjust after awhile. All we did was to try to pick you up, until we knew it was impossible."

"Until Sis tipped off the Government men," Dan added. Hawkes could imagine what their reaction had been to having a man with his power running wild. He was surprised that they had bothered to make even an attempt to see that he wasn't harmed.

He shrugged helplessly. "And where does it leave us now—beyond this hole in the ground?"

"The Government's put about fifty specialists on the notes you and Meinzer left," Dan answered, but there was no assurance in his voice. "They're trying to find some way to bring the psi factor under the control of your logical, rational mind."

He got to his knees and began crawling out of the little cave, while Hawkes tried to help Ellen follow him. Outside, Dan knocked off the dirt from his clothes and headed for the sedan he'd somehow gotten off the roof.

Hawkes followed, for want of anything better to do.

He knew the answers now—and he was worse off than ever. Instead of a horde of outside aliens, he had one single monster in his own skull, where he could never fight it, or even hope to escape it.

The power had been meant as a hope for the world. A man who could work such seeming miracles might have ended the threat of war; he'd have been the perfect spy, or better at attack than a hundred hydrogen bombs that had to smash whole cities to remove a few men and weapons. But now the world was better off without him. So long as he still lived, there would be nothing but danger from the alien monster in his head. He had no idea of his limits—but he was sure that it could trigger the energies of the universe to move the whole world out of its orbit, if that seemed necessary for his personal survival!

VIII

HAWKES leaned forward cautiously as the gray sedan moved up Tenth Avenue. His finger found the gun in Dan's coat pocket, and he pulled it out stealthily.

He knew that the only answer for him was suicide. He had to destroy himself, since no one else could!

He propped it up, pointing at his head, and his thumb pressed back on the trigger, further and further, until he felt sure the smallest change, would set it off. Then he waited for the rough spot in the street or the sudden stop at a light that would do the trick before he could stop it.

The car lurched—and the gun suddenly vanished, leaving his hand empty.

His responses were too quick—and his mind wasn't waiting, once it knew there was danger. He slumped back on the rear seat, trying to think. Drugs were out—he knew his system could throw them off.

But he couldn't remove himself!

He lifted his wrist to his teeth, and bit down savagely. If he could sever an artery . . . Pain shot through him, and he stared down at the blood.

Then the blood was gone, and the wound was closing before his eyes, until only smooth flesh remained. His mind could juggle the cells back into their original form.

It would have to be sudden, complete death.

And no death was that sudden! For a fraction of a second, there'd be life left—and during that split second, the damage would be repaired, or he would be shifted from danger.

There was no way out—unless he could pull himself to another planet, or throw himself back into the dim past. But that would take voluntary control, and he knew now that hours of effort had shown him how impossible that was. He hadn't been able to lift a crumb of bread from the table deliberately, in his original tests after he had treated himself.

He was faced with a problem that had to be solved—and there was no possible solution that he could find.

No man could face that dilemma forever without going insane. Hawkes shuddered, trying to picture what would happen if he went mad, and the wild talents began operating at every whim of his crazed mind!

ELLEN shouted suddenly, grabbing for the wheel. Hawkes felt himself tense, and began lifting from the seat of the car. But there was no visible danger, and Dan was slowing to a halt at the curb. Hawkes' body dropped back slowly.

"Dan," Ellen was whispering hoarsely. "Dan, we can't. If we take him back, they'll find him, and they'll know what he can do. They'll kill him. Eventually, they'll kill Will!"

Hawkes started to protest,

but Dan's words cut him short.

"You're right, Sis. They'll wait their time, until he won't know when to expect it —and then they'll drop an H-bomb on him, if they have to. That's faster than any nerve impulse!"

He swung back to face Hawkes, reaching for the door of the car. "Get out, Will—and get as far away as you can. I'm not going to drive you to your death. They'll get you eventually, but I won't be the one to make it easier for them!"

Hawkes jerked. The old fear came back suddenly.

You can't escape! They'll get you. Run! GO!

He screamed, as the golden haze flickered again. He could wipe out the Earth, but he couldn't survive, then. He could move back in time, but it would only mean other dangers—no man could stay awake forever, and he was used to civilized living.

The haze hesitated, while the sense of danger mounted. Then it was gone, as if the beast in his head had found no answer.

Suddenly the gray sedan lifted again, to a height of fifty feet above the tallest building. It shot forward, hesitated, and came down softly on a deserted side-road in Central Park.

His mind felt as if it were going to split. Dan and Ellen stared at him speechlessly.

You can't survive alone! No power is enough by itself! They'll get you! You are your own death-sentence! RUN! DON'T RUN!

Hawkes put his hand to his splitting skull, trying to force words through the agonies of pain, while slow understanding began to reach him.

"Dan! The scientists . . . get me there!"

Then his mind seemed to clamp down on itself, and he was unconscious. He could protect himself from almost anything—except his own brain!

HE was conscious of no pain, but only of irritation. There was a needle in his arm, and he removed it!

He opened his eyes slowly, to find himself the center of a group of men, while a white-clothed doctor stood staring at an empty hand that must have held a hypodermic.

Ellen cried out suddenly, and ran to him, cradling his head in her hands. He found her arm with his own hand, and stroked it slowly.

"You've found the answer?" he asked. Then he nodded, while the weight that had lain on him so long began to lift. His voice was suddenly positive. "You found it!"

One of the men pushed forward, but Dan shook his head, and came over to stand beside the cot where Hawkes lay. "No, Will. They didn't find it—you did! You found what we should have known—your unconscious mind may be a wild beast, but it isn't insane. When it was shocked into realizing that it couldn't save you by itself, it looked for help from your consciousness. And then it knocked you out—knocked itself out—until we could work on you."

"I guessed it," Hawkes said slowly. "But in that case, a psychotic with his id out in the driver's seat should become normal when they lock him up. Or wait—maybe his unconsciousness is a bit insane. Maybe. But you still have to communicate with that unconscious part of the brain, to make it understand that it has to surrender. And all the psychiatrists have been driving themselves crazy trying to solve that!"

"Touché," an older man said, and there was a faint sound of amusement from some of the others. "But this psi factor *is* the means of communication! You told us that yourself, while you were undergoing our hastily improvised hypnotic education of your brain. It always has been. The minute a girl bothered with poltergeists finds she is the cause of them, they stop. It's a faint, weak channel between consciousness and unconsciousness—or subconsciousness, if you prefer. And yours was widened by the treatment, even if it wasn't ready to work yet. We simply used your own technique to improve the relationship. All you ever needed was a longer, harder treatment than you and Meinzer had given yourselves. You just stopped too soon."

HAWKES dropped back comfortably onto the cot. He reached out for a glass of water, lifted it to his lips, and put it back—without using his hands. He thought of his clothes, and they were suddenly on him, over the single white garment he had been wearing. Another thought took that away, to leave him normally dressed.

Whether they were entirely correct or not in their theories, the psi factor was no longer wild. He had it under full control!

He sat up, just as three men

entered the crowded room. One wore the uniform of a four-star general, but the familiar faces of the two civilians told Hawkes at once that they were more important than any general could be.

He was about to become officially the National Arsenal and replacement for all the armies, navies, and air-corps they had ever dreamed of having. He'd also become their bridge into space, their means of solving the secrets of the planets, and probably their chief historical tool, since nothing could ever be secret from him.

It was going to be a busy life for him and for the others like him who would now be carefully selected and treated!

He grinned faintly, as he realized that they didn't know yet just how important he was. He wasn't going to be a National Resource—he'd be a World Resource. This power was too great for any local political use, and no man who had it along with the full correlation of his conscious and subconscious mind could ever see it any other way.

But right now, he had other pressing business. He grinned at Ellen. "You don't mind a small wedding, do you?" he asked.

She shook her head, beginning to smile. He reached for her hand. This psi factor was going to be a handy thing to have around, with its complete control of space and time.

"I'm taking a two-week honeymoon before we talk business," he told the approaching three men. "But don't go away. We'll be back in ten minutes!"

Honolulu looked lovely in the moonlight, and June was the perfect month for a wedding.

EDITORIAL NOTE: Actually, *Pursuit* ends where the real story is just beginning! Disregarding other powers, when men can move instantly over any distance by simple desire, it's the beginning of a life and culture totally unrelated to anything we know. What will it be like? Where should houses be built—and will they be built? A housewife can have her dining-room in the mountains and her kitchen in a community (to simplify and cheapen plumbing, etc.) 10,000 miles away, or on another planet! There can be no national boundaries, of course. What happens to the multiplicity of languages? What happens to government? How do you catch a criminal? How do you hold him?

There are endless possibilities, naturally. We're tossing it open to the readers. You tell us what you think that world will be like—if you can! We'll print the best letters—and if the authors want to use this background, we'll buy the best stories based on it.

We will not be responsible for mental break-downs, however!

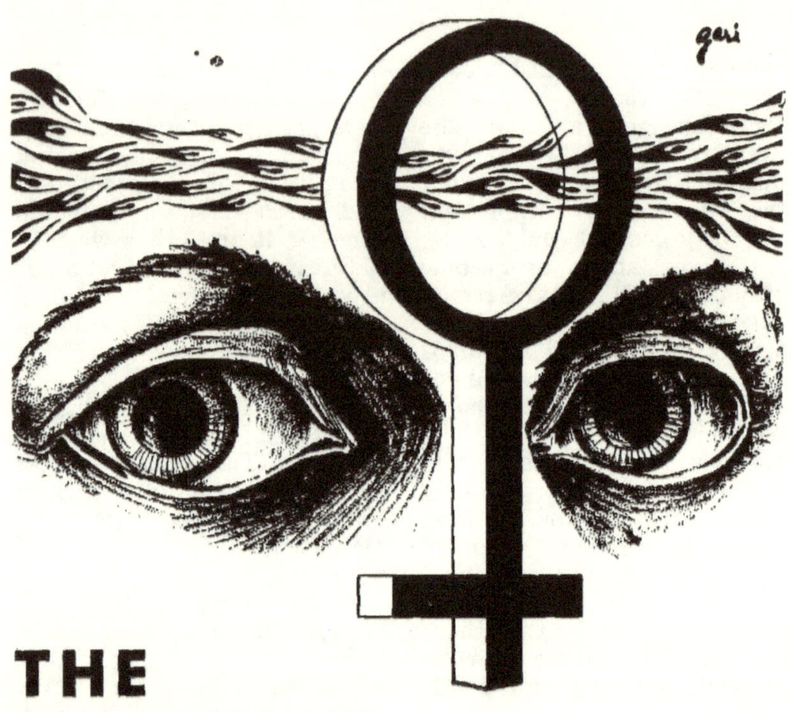

THE ULTROOM ERROR

by JERRY SOHL

Smith admitted he had made an error involving a few murders—and a few thousand years. He was entitled to a sense of humor, though, even in the Ultroom!

HB73782. Ultroom error. Tendal 13. Arvid 6. Kanad transfer out of 1609 complete, intact, but too near limit of 1,000 days. Next Kanad transfer ready. 1951. Reginald, son of Mr. and Mrs. Martin Laughton, 3495 Orland Drive, Marionville, Illinois, U. S. A. Arrive his 378th day. TB-73782.

NANCY LAUGHTON sat on the blanket she had spread on the lawn in her front yard, knitting a pair of booties for the PTA bazaar. Occasionally she glanced at her son in the play pen, who was getting his daily dose of sunshine. He was gurgling happily, examining a ball, a cheese grater and a linen baby book, all with perfunctory interest.

When she looked up again she noticed a man walking by—except he turned up the walk and crossed the lawn to her.

He was a little taller than her husband, had piercing blue eyes and a rather amused set to his lips.

"Hello, Nancy," he said.

"Hello, Joe," she answered. It was her brother who lived in Kankakee.

"I'm going to take the baby for a while," he said.

"All right, Joe."

He reached into the pen, picked up the baby. As he did so the baby's knees hit the side of the play pen and young Laughton let out a scream—half from hurt and half from sudden lack of confidence in his new handler. But this did not deter Joe. He started off with the child.

Around the corner and after the man came a snarling mongrel dog, eyes bright, teeth glinting in the sunlight. The man did not turn as the dog threw himself at him, burying his teeth in his leg. Surprised, the man dropped the screaming child on the lawn and turned to the dog. Joe seemed off balance and he backed up confusedly in the face of the snapping jaws. Then he suddenly turned and walked away, the dog at his heels.

"I tell you, the man said he was my brother and he made me think he was," Nancy told her husband for the tenth time. "I don't even have a brother."

Martin Laughton sighed. "I can't understand why you believed him. It's just—just plain nuts, Nancy!"

"Don't you think I know it?" Nancy said tearfully. "I feel like I'm going crazy. I can't say I dreamt it because there was Reggie with his bleeding knees, squalling for all he was worth on the grass—Oh, I don't even want to think about it."

"We haven't lost Reggie, Nancy, remember that. Now why don't you try to get some rest?"

"You—you don't believe me at all, do you, Martin?"

When her husband did not answer, her head sank to her

arms on the table and she sobbed.

"Nancy, for heaven's sake, of course I believe you. I'm trying to think it out, that's all. We should have called the police."

Nancy shook her head in her arms. "They'd—never—believe me either," she moaned.

"I'd better go and make sure Reggie's all right." Martin got up out of his chair and went to the stairs.

"I'm going with you," Nancy said, hurriedly rising and coming over to him.

"We'll go up and look at him together."

They found Reggie peacefully asleep in his crib in his room upstairs. They checked the windows and tucked in the blankets. They paused in the room for a moment and then Martin stole his arm around his wife and led her to the door.

"As I've said, sergeant, this fellow hypnotized my wife. He made her think he was her brother. She doesn't even have a brother. Then he tried to get away with the baby." Martin leaned down and patted the dog. "It was Tiger here who scared him off."

The police sergeant looked at the father, at Nancy and then at the dog. He scribbled notes in his book.

"Are you a rich man, Mr. Laughton?" he asked.

"Not at all. The bank still owns most of the house. I have a few hundred dollars, that's all."

"What do you do?"

"Office work, mostly. I'm a junior executive in an insurance company."

"Any enemies?"

"No . . . Oh, I suppose I have a few people I don't get along with, like anybody else. Nobody who'd do anything like this, though."

The sergeant flipped his notebook closed. "You'd better keep your dog inside and around the kid as much as possible. Keep your doors and windows locked. I'll see that the prowl car keeps an eye on the house. Call us if anything seems unusual or out of the way."

Nancy had taken a sedative and was asleep by the time Martin finished cleaning the .30-.30 rifle he used for deer hunting. He put it by the stairs, ready for use, fully loaded, leaning it against the wall next to the telephone stand.

THE front door bell rang. He answered it. It was Dr. Stuart and another man.

"I came as soon as I could, Martin," the young doctor said, stepping inside with the other man. "This is my new assistant, Dr. Tompkins."

Martin and Tompkins shook hands.

"The baby—?" Dr. Stuart asked.

"Upstairs," Martin said.

"You'd better get him, Dr. Tompkins, if we're to take him to the hospital. I'll stay here with Mr. Laughton. How've you been, Martin?"

"Fine."

"How's everything at the office?"

"Fine."

"And your wife?"

"She's fine, too."

"Glad to hear it, Martin. Mighty glad. Say, by the way, there's that bill you owe me. I think it's $32, isn't that right?"

"Yes, I'd almost forgotten about it."

"Why don't you be a good fellow and write a check for it? It's been over a year, you know."

"That's right. I'll get right at it." Martin went over to his desk, opened it and started looking for his checkbook. Dr. Stuart stood by him, making idle comment until Dr. Tompkins came down the stairs with the sleeping baby cuddled against his shoulder.

"Never mind the check, now, Martin. I see we're ready to go." He went over to his assistant and took the baby. Together they walked out the front door.

"Good-bye," Martin said, going to the door.

Then he was nearly bowled over by the discharge of the .30-.30. Dr. Stuart crumpled to the ground, the baby falling to the lawn. Dr. Tompkins whirled and there was a second shot. Dr. Tompkins pitched forward on his face.

The figure of a woman ran from the house, retrieved the now squalling infant and ran back into the house. Once inside, Nancy slammed the door, gave the baby to the stunned Martin and headed for the telephone.

"One of them was the same man!" she cried.

Martin gasped, sinking into a chair with the baby. "I believed them," he said slowly and uncomprehendingly. "They made me believe them!"

"Those bodies," the sergeant said. "Would you mind pointing them out to me, please?"

"Aren't they—aren't they on the walk?" Mrs. Laughton asked.

"There is nothing on the walk, Mrs. Laughton."

"But there *must* be! I tell you I shot these men who posed as doctors. One of them was the same man who tried to take the baby this afternoon. They hypnotized my husband—"

"Yes, I know, Mrs. Laughton. We've been through that." The sergeant went to the door and opened it. "Say, Homer, take another look around the walk and the bushes. There's supposed to be two of them. Shot with a .30-.30."

He turned and picked up the gun and examined it again. "Ever shoot a gun before, Mrs. Laughton?"

"Many times. Martin and I used to go hunting together before we had Reggie."

The sergeant nodded. "You were taking an awful chance, shooting at a guy carrying your baby, don't you think?"

"I shot him in the legs. The other—the other turned and I shot him in the chest. I could even see his eyes when he turned around. If I hadn't pulled the trigger then . . . I don't want to remember it."

The patrolman pushed the door open. "There's no bodies out here but there's some blood. Quite a lot of blood. A little to one side of the walk."

The policemen went out.

"Thank God you woke up, Nancy," Martin said. "I'd have let them have the baby." He reached over and smoothed the sleeping Reggie's hair.

Nancy, who was rocking the boy, narrowed her eyes.

"I wonder why they want our baby? He's just like any other baby. We don't have any money. We couldn't pay a ransom."

"Reggie's pretty cute, though," Martin said. "You will have to admit that."

Nancy smiled. Then she suddenly stopped rocking.

"Martin!"

He sat up quickly.

"Where's Tiger?"

Together they rose and walked around the room. They found him in a corner, eyes open, tongue protruding. He was dead.

"IF we keep Reggie in the house much longer he'll turn out to be a hermit," Martin said at breakfast a month later. "He needs fresh air and sunshine."

"I'm not going to sit on the lawn alone with him, Martin. I just can't, that's all. I'd be able to think of nothing but that day."

"Still thinking about it? I think we'd have heard from them again if they were coming back. They probably got somebody else's baby by this time." Martin finished his coffee and rose to kiss her goodbye. "But for safety's sake I guess you'd better keep that gun handy."

The morning turned into a brilliant, sunshiny day. Puffs of clouds moved slowly across the summer sky and a warm breeze rustled the trees. It would be a crime to keep Reggie inside on a day like this, Nancy thought.

So she called Mrs. MacDougal, the next door neighbor. Mrs. MacDougal was familiar with what had happened to the Laughtons and she agreed to keep an eye on Nancy and Reggie and to call the police at the first sign of trouble.

With a fearful but determined heart Nancy moved the play pen and set it up in the front yard. She spread a blanket for herself and put Reggie in the pen. Her heart pounded all the while and she watched the street for any strangers, ready to flee inside if need be. Reggie just gurgled with delight at the change in environment.

THIS peaceful scene was disturbed by a speeding car in which two men were riding. The car roared up the street, swerved toward the parkway, tires screaming, bounced over the curb and sidewalk, straight toward the child and mother. Reggie, attracted by the sudden noise, looked up to see the approaching vehicle. His mother stood up, set her palms against her cheeks and shrieked.

The car came on, crunched over the play pen, killing the child. The mother was hit and instantly killed, force of the blow snapping her spine and tossing her against the house. The car plunged on into a tree, hitting it a terrible blow, crumbling the car's forward end so it looked like an accordion. The men were thrown from the machine.

"We'll never be able to prosecute in this case," the states attorney said. "At least not on a drunken driving basis."

"I can't get over it," the chief of police said. "I've got at least six men who will swear the man was drunk. He staggered, reeled and gave the usual drunk talk. He reeked of whiskey."

The prosecutor handed the report over the desk. "Here's the analysis. Not a trace of alcohol. He couldn't have even had a smell of near beer. Here's another report. This is his physical exam made not long afterwards. The man was in perfect health. Only variations are he had a scar on his leg where something, probably a dog, bit him once. And then a scar on his chest. It looked like an old gunshot wound, they said. Must have happened years ago."

"That's odd. The man who accosted Mrs. Laughton in the afternoon was bitten by their dog. Later that night she said she shot the same man in the chest. Since the scars are healed it obviously couldn't be the same man. But there's a real coincidence for you. And speaking of the dogbite, the Laughton dog died that night. His menu evidently didn't agree with him. Never did figure what killed him, actually."

"Any record of treatment on the man she shot?"

"The *men*. You'll remember, there were two. No, we never found a trace of either. No doctor ever made a report of a gunshot wound that night. No hospital had a case either—at least not within several hundred miles—that night or several nights afterwards. Ever been shot with .30-.30?"

The state attorney shook his head. "I wouldn't be here if I had."

"I'll say you wouldn't. The pair must have crawled away to die God knows where."

"Getting back to the man who ran over the child and killed Mrs. Laughton. Why did he pretend to be drunk?"

It was the chief's turn to shake his head. "Your guess is as good as mine. There are a lot of angles to this case none of us understand. It looks deliberate, but where's the motive?"

"What does the man have to say?"

"I was afraid you'd get to him," the chief said, his neck reddening. "It's all been rather embarrassing to the department." He coughed self-consciously. "He's proved a strange one, all right. He says his name is John Smith and he's got cards to prove it, too—for example, a social security card. It looks authentic, yet there's no such number on file in Washington, so we've discovered. We've had him in jail for a week and we've all taken turns questioning him. He laughs and admits his guilt—in fact, he seems amused by most everything. Sometimes all alone in his cell he'll start laughing for no apparent reason. It gives you the creeps."

THE states attorney leaned back in his chair. "Maybe it's a case for an alienist."

"One jump ahead of you.

Dr. Stone thinks he's normal, but won't put down any I.Q. Actually, he can't figure him out himself. Smith seems to take delight in answering questions—sort of anticipates them and has the answer ready before you're half through asking."

"Well, if Dr. Stone says he's normal, that's enough for me." The prosecutor was silent for a moment. Then, "How about the husband?"

"Laughton? We're afraid to let him see him. All broken up. No telling what kind of a rumpus he'd start—especially if Smith started his funny business."

"Guess you're right. Well, Mr. Smith won't think it's so funny when we hang criminal negligence or manslaughter on him. By the way, you've checked possible family connections?"

"Nobody ever saw John Smith before. Even at the address on his driver's license. And there's no duplicate of that in Springfield, in case you're interested."

The man who had laughingly told police his name was John Smith lay on his cot in the county jail, his eyes closed, his arms folded across his chest. This gave him the appearance of being alert despite reclining. Even as he lay, his mouth held a hint of a smile.

Arvid 6—for John Smith *was* Arvid 6—had lain in that position for more than four hours, when suddenly he snapped his eyes open and appeared to be listening. For a moment a look of concern crossed his face and he swung his legs to the floor and sat there expectantly. Arvid 6 knew Tendal 13 had materialized and was somewhere in the building.

Eventually there were some sounds from beyond the steel cell and doorway. There was a clang when the outer doorway was opened and Arvid 6 rose from his cot.

"Your lawyer's here to see you," the jailer said, indicating the man with the brief case. "Ring the buzzer when you're through." The jailer let the man in, locked the cell door and walked away.

The man threw the brief case on the jail cot and stood glaring.

"Your damned foolishness has gone far enough. I'm sick and tired of it," he declared. "If you carry on any more we'll never get back to the Ultroom!"

"I'm sorry, Tendal," the man on the cot said. "I didn't think—"

"You're absolutely right.

You didn't think. Crashing that car into that tree and killing that woman—that was the last straw. You don't even deserve to get back to our era. You ought to be made to rot here."

"I'm *really* sorry about that," Arvid 6 said.

"YOU know the instructions. Just because you work in the Ultroom don't get to thinking human life doesn't have any value. We wouldn't be here if it hadn't. But to unnecessarily kill—" The older man shook his head. "You could have killed yourself as well and we'd never get the job done. As it is, you almost totally obliterated me." Tendal 13 paced the length of the cell and back again, gesturing as he talked.

"It was only with the greatest effort I pulled myself back together again. I doubt that you could have done it. And then all the while you've been sitting here, probably enjoying yourself with your special brand of humor I have grown to despise."

"You didn't have to come along at all, you know," Arvid 6 said.

"How well I know! How sorry I am that I ever did! It was only because I was sorry for you, because someone older and more experienced than you was needed. I volunteered. Imagine that! I volunteered! Tendal 13 reaches the height of stupidity and volunteers to help Arvid 6 go back 6,000 years to bring Kanad back, to correct a mistake Arvid 6 made!" He snorted. "I still can't believe I was ever that stupid. I only prove it when I pinch myself and here I am.

"Oh, you've been a joy to be with! First it was that hunt in ancient Mycenae when you let the lion escape the hunters' quaint spears and we were partly eaten by the lion in the bargain, although you dazzled the hunters, deflecting their spears. And then your zest for drink when we were with Octavian in Alexandria that led to everybody's amusement but ours when we were ambushed by Anthony's men. And worst of all, that English barmaid you became engrossed with at our last stop in 1609, when her husband mistook me for you and you let him take me apart piece by piece—"

"All right, all right," Arvid 6 said. "I'll admit I've made some mistakes. You're just not adventurous, that's all."

"Shut up! For once you're going to listen to me. Our instructions specifically stated we were to have as little as possible to do with these people. But at every turn you've got us more and more enmeshed with them. If that's adventure, you can have it."

Tendal 13 sat down wearily and sank his head in his hands. "It was you who conceived the idea of taking Reggie right out of his play pen. 'Watch me take that child right out from under its mother's nose' were your exact words. And before I could stop you, you did. Only you forgot an important factor in the equation—the dog, Tiger. And you nursed a dogbite most of the afternoon before it healed. And then you took your spite out on the poor thing by suggesting suffocation to it that night.

"And speaking of that night, you remember we agreed I was to do the talking. But no, you pulled a switch and captured Martin Laughton's attention. 'I came as soon as I could, Martin,' you said. And suddenly I played a very minor role. 'This is my new assistant, Dr. Tompkins,' you said. And then what happened? I get shot in the legs and you get a hole in your back. We were both nearly obliterated that time and we didn't even come close to getting the child.

"Still you wanted to run the whole show. 'I'm younger than you,' you said. 'I'll take the wheel.' And the next thing I know I'm floating in space halfway to nowhere with two broken legs, a spinal injury, concussion and some of the finest bruises you ever saw."

"THESE twentieth century machines aren't what they ought to be," Arvid 6 said.

"You never run out of excuses, do you, Arvid? Remember what you said in the Ultroom when you pushed the lever clear over and transferred Kanad back 6,000 years? 'My hand slipped.' As simple as that. 'My hand slipped.' It was so simple everyone believed you. You were given no real punishment. In a way it was a reward—at least to you—getting to go back and rescue the life germ of Kanad out of each era he'd be born in."

Tendal 13 turned and looked steadily and directly at Arvid 6. "Do you know what I think? I think you deliberately pushed the lever over as far as it would go *just to see what would happen.* That's how simple I think it was."

Arvid 6 flushed, turned away and looked at the floor.

"What crazy things have you been doing since I've been gone?" Tendal 13 asked.

Arvid 6 sighed. "After what you just said I guess it wouldn't amuse you, although it has me. They got to me right after the accident before I had a chance to collect my wits, dematerialize or anything—you said we shouldn't dematerialize in front of anybody."

"That's right."

"Well, I didn't know what to do. I could see they thought I was drunk, so I was. But they had a blood sample before I could manufacture any alcohol in my blood, although I implanted a memory in them that I reeked of it." He laughed. "I fancy they're thoroughly confused."

"And you're thoroughly amused, no doubt. Have they questioned you?"

"At great length. They had a psychiatrist in to see me. He was a queer fellow with the most stupid set of questions and tests I ever saw."

"And you amused yourself with him."

"I suppose you'd think so."

"Who do you tell them you are?"

"John Smith. A rather prevalent name here, I understand. I manufactured a pasteboard called a social security card and a driver's license—"

"Never mind. It's easy to see you've been your own inimitable self. Believe me, if I ever get back to the Ultroom I hope I never see you again. And I hope I'll never leave there again though I'm rejuvenated through a million years."

"Was Kanad's life germ transferred all right this time?"

Tendal 13 shook his head. "I haven't heard. The transfers are getting more difficult all the time. In 1609, you'll remember, it was a case of pneumonia for the two-year-old. A simple procedure. It wouldn't work here. Medicine's too far along." He produced a notebook. "The last jump was 342 years, a little more than average. The next ought to be around 2250. Things will be more difficult than ever there, probably."

"Do you think Kanad will be angry about all this?"

"How would you like to have to go through all those birth processes, to have your life germ knocked from one era to the next?"

"Frankly, I didn't think he'd go back so far."

"If it had been anybody but Kanad nobody'd ever have thought of going back after it. The life germ of the head of the whole galactic system who came to the Ultroom to be transplanted to a younger body—and then sending him back beyond his original birth date—" Tendal 13 got up and commenced his pacing again. "Oh, I suppose Kanad's partly to blame, wanting rejuvenating at only 300 years. Some have waited a thousand or more or until their bones are like paper."

"I just wonder how angry Kanad will be," Arvid muttered.

HB92167. Ultroom Error. Tendal 13. Arvid 6. Kanad transfer out of 1951 complete. Next Kanad transfer ready. 2267. Phullam 19, son of Orla 39 and Rhoda R, 22H Level M, Hemisphere B, Quadrant 3, Sector I. Arrive his 329th Day.

TB92167

ARVID 6 rose from the cot and the two men faced each other.

"Before we leave, Arvid," Tendal 13 started to say.

"I know, I know. You want me to let you handle everything."

"Exactly. Is that too much to ask after all you've done?"

"I guess I have made mistakes. From now on you be the boss. I'll do whatever you say."

"I hope I can count on that." Tendal 13 rang the jail buzzer.

The jailer unlocked the cell door.

"You remember the chief said it's all right to take him with me, Matthews," Tendal 13 told the jailer.

"Yes, I remember," the jailer said mechanically, letting them both out of the cell.

They walked together down the jail corridor. When they came to another barred door the jailer fumbled with the keys and clumsily tried several with no luck.

Arvid 6, an amused set to his mouth and devilment in his eyes, watched the jailer's expression as he walked through the bars of the door. He laughed as he saw the jailer's eyes bulge.

"Arvid!"

Tendal 13 walked briskly through the door, snatched Arvid 6 by the shoulders and shook him.

The jailer watched stupified as the two men vanished in the middle of a violent argument.

YOUTH

by ISAAC ASIMOV

Red and Slim found the two strange little animals the morning after they heard the thunder sounds. They knew that they could never show their new pets to their parents.

THERE was a spatter of pebbles against the window and the youngster stirred in his sleep. Another, and he was awake.

He sat up stiffly in bed. Seconds passed while he interpreted his strange surroundings. He wasn't in his own home, of course. This was out in the country. It was colder than it should be and

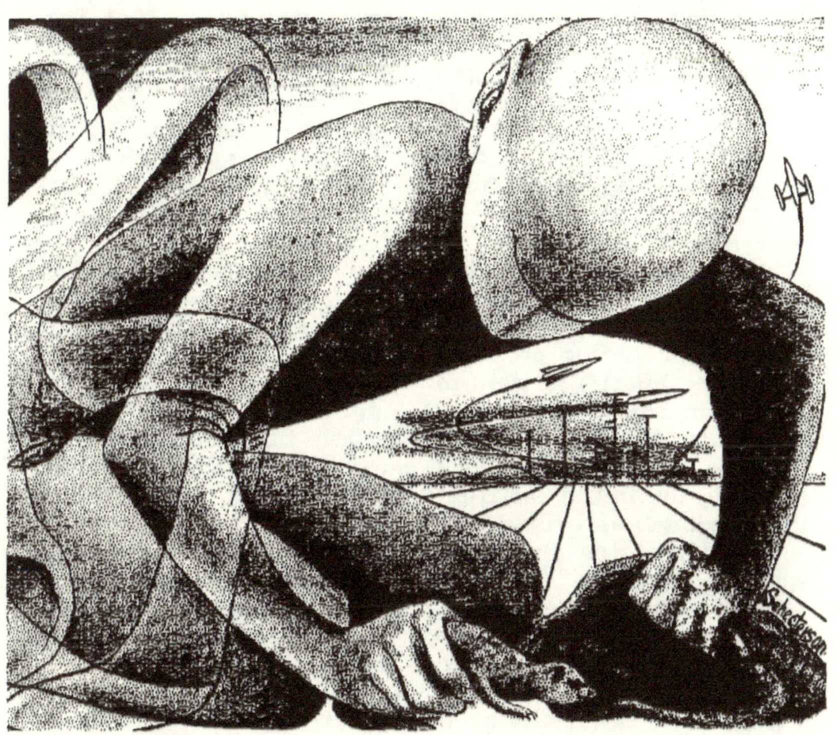

there was green at the window.

"Slim!"

The call was a hoarse, urgent whisper, and the youngster bounded to the open window.

Slim wasn't his real name, but the new friend he had met the day before had needed only one look at his slight figure to say, "You're Slim." He added, "I'm Red."

Red wasn't his real name, either, but its appropriateness was obvious. They were friends instantly with the quick unquestioning friendship of young ones not yet quite in adolescence, before even the first stains of adulthood began to make their appearance.

Slim cried, "Hi, Red!" and waved cheerfully, still blinking the sleep out of himself.

Red kept to his croaking whisper, "Quiet! You want to wake somebody?"

Slim noticed all at once that the sun scarcely topped the low hills in the east that the shadows were long and soft and that the grass was wet.

Slim said, more softly, "What's the matter?"

Red only waved for him to come out.

Slim dressed quickly, gladly confining his morning wash to the momentary sprinkle of a little luke-warm water. He let the air dry the exposed portions of his body as he ran out, while bare skin grew wet against the dewy grass.

Red said, "You've got to be quiet. If Mom wakes up or Dad or your Dad or even any of the hands then it'll be 'Come on in or you'll catch your death of cold.' "

He mimicked voice and tone faithfully, so that Slim laughed and thought that there had never been so funny a fellow as Red.

Slim said, eagerly, "Do you come out here every day like this, Red? Real early? It's like the whole world is just yours, isn't it, Red? No one else around and all like that." He felt proud at being allowed entrance into this private world.

Red stared at him sidelong. He said carelessly, "I've been up for hours. Didn't you hear it last night?"

"Hear what?"

"Thunder."

"Was there a thunder storm?" Slim never slept through a thunderstorm.

"I guess not. But there was thunder. I heard it, and then I went to the window and it wasn't raining. It was all stars and the sky was just getting sort of almost gray. You know what I mean?"

Slim had never seen it so, but he nodded.

"So I just thought I'd go out," said Red.

They walked along the grassy side of the concrete road that split the panorama right down the middle all the way down to where it vanished among the hills. It was so old that Red's father couldn't tell Red when it had been built. It didn't have a crack or a rough spot in it.

Red said, "Can you keep a secret?"

"Sure, Red. What kind of a secret?"

"Just a secret. Maybe I'll tell you and maybe I won't. I don't know yet." Red broke a long, supple stem from a fern they passed, methodically stripped it of its leaflets and swung what was left whip-fashion. For a moment, he was on a wild charger, which reared and champed under his iron control. Then he got tired, tossed the whip aside and stowed the charger away in a corner of his imagination for future use.

He said, "There'll be a circus around."

Slim said, "That's no secret. I knew that. My Dad told me even before we came here—"

"That's not the secret. Fine secret! Ever see a circus?"

"Oh, sure. You bet."

"Like it?"

"Say, there isn't anything I like better."

Red was watching out of the corner of his eyes again. "Ever think you would like to be with a circus? I mean, for good?"

Slim considered, "I guess not. I think I'll be an astronomer like my Dad. I think he wants me to be."

"Huh! Astronomer!" said Red.

Slim felt the doors of the new, private world closing on him and astronomy became a thing of dead stars and black, empty space.

He said, placatingly, "A circus *would* be more fun."

"You're just saying that."

"No, I'm not. I mean it."

Red grew argumentative. "Suppose you had a chance to join the circus right now. What would you do?"

"I—I—"

"See!" Red affected scornful laughter.

Slim was stung. "I'd join up."

"Go on."

"Try me."

Red whirled at him, strange and intense. "You meant that? You want to go in with me?"

"What do you mean?" Slim stepped back a bit, surprised by the unexpected challenge.

"I got something that can get us into the circus. Maybe someday we can even have a circus of our own. We could be the biggest circus-fellows in the world. That's if you want to go in with me. Otherwise—Well, I guess I can do it on my own. I just thought: Let's give good old Slim a chance."

The world was strange and glamorous, and Slim said. "Sure thing, Red. I'm in! What is it, huh, Red? Tell me what it is."

"Figure it out. What's the most important thing in circuses?"

Slim thought desperately He wanted to give the right answer. Finally, he said, "Acrobats?"

"Holy Smokes! I wouldn't go five steps to look at acrobats."

"I don't know then."

"Animals, that's what! What's the best side-show? Where are the biggest crowds? Even in the main rings the best acts are animal acts." There was no doubt in Red's voice.

"Do you think so?"

"Everyone thinks so. You ask anyone. Anyway, I found

animals this morning. Two of them."

"And you've got them?"

"Sure. That's the secret. Are you telling?"

"Of course not."

"Okay. I've got them in the barn. Do you want to see them?"

They were almost at the barn; its huge open door black. Too black. They had been heading there all the time. Slim stopped in his tracks.

He tried to make his words casual. "Are they big?"

"Would I fool with them if they were big? They can't hurt you. They're only about so long. I've got them in a cage."

They were in the barn now and Slim saw the large cage suspended from a hook in the roof. It was covered with stiff canvas.

Red said, "We used to have some bird there or something. Anyway, they can't get away from there. Come on, let's go up to the loft."

They clambered up the wooden stairs and Red hooked the cage toward them.

Slim pointed and said, "There's sort of a hole in the canvas."

Red frowned. "How'd that get there?" He lifted the canvas, looked in, and said, with relief, "They're still there."

"The canvas appeared to be burned," worried Slim.

"You want to look, or don't you?"

Slim nodded slowly. He wasn't sure he wanted to, after all. They might be—

But the canvas had been jerked off and there they were. Two of them, the way Red said. They were small, and sort of disgusting-looking. The animals moved quickly as the canvas lifted and were on the side toward the youngsters. Red poked a cautious finger at them.

"Watch out," said Slim, in agony.

"They don't hurt you," said Red. "Ever see anything like them?"

"No."

"Can't you see how a circus would jump at a chance to have these?"

"Maybe they're too small for a circus."

Red looked annoyed. He let go the cage which swung back and forth pendulum-fashion. "You're just trying to back out, aren't you?"

"No, I'm not. It's just—"

"They're not too small, don't worry. Right now, I've only got one worry."

"What's that?"

"Well, I've got to keep them till the circus comes, don't I?

I've got to figure out what to feed them meanwhile."

The cage swung and the little trapped creatures clung to its bars, gesturing at the youngsters with queer, quick motions—almost as though they were intelligent.

II

THE Astronomer entered the dining room with decorum. He felt very much the guest.

He said, "Where are the youngsters? My son isn't in his room."

The Industrialist smiled. "They've been out for hours. However, breakfast was forced into them among the women some time ago, so there is nothing to worry about. Youth, Doctor, youth!"

"Youth!" The word seemed to depress the Astronomer.

They ate breakfast in silence. The Industrialist said once, "You really think they'll come. The day looks so—*normal.*"

The Astronomer said, "They'll come."

That was all.

Afterward the Industrialist said, "You'll pardon me. I can't conceive your playing so elaborate a hoax. You really spoke to them?"

"As I speak to you. At least, in a sense. They can project thoughts."

"I gathered that must be so from your letter. How, I wonder."

"I could not say. I asked them and, of course, they were vague. Or perhaps it was just that I could not understand. It involves a projector for the focussing of thought and, even more than that, conscious attention on the part of both projector and receptor. It was quite a while before I realized they were trying to think at me. Such thought-projectors may be part of the science they will give us."

"Perhaps," said the Industrialist. "Yet think of the changes it would bring to society. A thought-projector!"

"Why not? Change would be good for us."

"I don't think so."

"It is only in old age that change is unwelcome," said the Astronomer, "and races can be old as well as individuals."

The Industrialist pointed out the window. "You see that road. It was built Beforethewars. I don't know exactly when. It is as good now as the day it was built. We couldn't possibly duplicate it now. The race was young when that was built, eh?"

"Then? Yes! At least they

weren't afraid of new things."

"No. I wish they had been. Where is the society of Beforethewars? Destroyed, Doctor! What good were youth and new things? We are better off now. The world is peaceful and jogs along. The race goes nowhere but after all, there is nowhere to go. *They* proved that. The men who built the road. I will speak with your visitors as I agreed, if they come. But I think I will only ask them to go."

"The race is not going nowhere," said the Astronomer, earnestly. "It is going toward final destruction. My university has a smaller student body each year. Fewer books are written. Less work is done. An old man sleeps in the sun and his days are peaceful and unchanging, but each day finds him nearer death all the same."

"Well, well," said the Industrialist.

"No, don't dismiss it. Listen. Before I wrote you, I investigated your position in the planetary economy."

"And you found me solvent?" interrupted the Industrialist, smiling.

"Why, yes. Oh, I see, you are joking. And yet—perhaps the joke is not far off. You are less solvent than your father and he was less solvent than his father. Perhaps your son will no longer be solvent. It becomes too troublesome for the planet to support even the industries that still exist, though they are toothpicks to the oak trees of Beforethewars. We will be back to village economy and then to what? The caves?"

"And the infusion of fresh technological knowledge will be the changing of all that?"

"Not just the new knowledge. Rather the whole effect of change, of a broadening of horizons. Look, sir, I chose you to approach in this matter not only because you were rich and influential with government officials, but because you had an unusual reputation, for these days, of daring to break with tradition. Our people will resist change and you would know how to handle them, how to see to it that—that—"

"That the youth of the race is revived?"

"Yes."

"With its atomic bombs?"

"The atomic bombs," returned the Astronomer, "need not be the end of civilization. These visitors of mine had their atomic bomb, or whatever their equivalent was on their own worlds, and survived it, because they didn't

give up. Don't you see? It wasn't the bomb that defeated us, but our own shellshock. This may be the last chance to reverse the process."

"Tell me," said the Industrialist, "what do these friends from space want in return?"

The Astronomer hesitated. He said, "I will be truthful with you. They come from a denser planet. Ours is richer in the lighter atoms."

"They want magnesium? Aluminum?"

"No, sir. Carbon and hydrogen. They want coal and oil."

"Really?"

The Astronomer said, quickly, "You are going to ask why creatures who have mastered space travel, and therefore atomic power, would want coal and oil. I can't answer that."

The Industrialist smiled, "But I can. This is the best evidence yet of the truth of your story. Superficially, atomic power would seem to preclude the use of coal and oil. However, quite apart from the energy gained by their combustion they remain, and always will remain, the basic raw material for all organic chemistry. Plastics, dyes, pharmaceuticals, solvents. Industry could not exist without them, even in an atomic age. Still, if coal and oil are the low price for which they would sell us the troubles and tortures of racial youth, my answer is that the commodity would be dear if offered gratis."

The Astronomer sighed and said, "There are the boys!"

They were visible through the open window, standing together in the grassy field and lost in animated conversation. The Industrialist's son pointed imperiously and the Astronomer's son nodded and made off at a run toward the house.

The Industrialist said, "There is the Youth you speak of. Our race has as much of it as it ever had."

"Yes, but we age them quickly and pour them into the mold."

Slim scuttled into the room, the door banging behind him.

The Astronomer said, in mild disapproval, "What's this?"

Slim looked up in surprise and came to a halt. "I beg your pardon. I didn't know anyone was here. I am sorry to have interrupted." His enunciation was almost painfully precise.

The Industrialist said, "It's all right, youngster."

But the Astronomer said, "Even if you had been entering an empty room, son, there would be no cause for slamming a door."

"Nonsense," insisted the Industrialist. "The youngster has done no harm. You simply scold him for being young. You, with your views!"

He said to Slim, "Come here, lad."

Slim advanced slowly.

"How do you like the country, eh?"

"Very much, sir, thank you."

"My son has been showing you about the place, has he?"

"Yes, sir. Red—I mean—"

"No, no. Call him Red. I call him that myself. Now tell me, what are you two up to, eh?"

Slim looked away. "Why—just exploring, sir."

The Industrialist turned to the Astronomer. "There you are, youthful curiosity and adventure-lust. The race has not yet lost it."

Slim said, "Sir?"

"Yes, lad."

The youngster took a long time in getting on with it. He said, "Red sent me in for something good to eat, but I don't exactly know what he meant. I didn't like to say so."

"Why, just ask cook. She'll have something good for young'uns to eat."

"Oh, no, sir. I mean for animals."

"For animals?"

"Yes, sir. What do animals eat?"

The Astronomer said, "I am afraid my son is city-bred."

"Well," said the Industrialist, "there's no harm in that. What kind of an animal, lad?"

"A small one, sir."

"Then try grass or leaves, and if they don't want that, nuts or berries would probably do the trick."

"Thank you, sir." Slim ran out again, closing the door gently behind him.

The Astronomer said, "Do you suppose they've trapped an animal alive?" He was obviously perturbed.

"That's common enough. There's no shooting on my estate and it's tame country, full of rodents and small creatures. Red is always coming home with pets of one sort or another. They rarely maintain his interest for long."

He looked at the wall clock. "Your friends should have been here by now, shouldn't they?"

III

THE swaying had come to a halt and it was dark. The Explorer was not comfortable in the alien air. It felt as thick as soup and he had to breath shallowly. Even so—

He reached out in a sudden need for company. The Merchant was warm to the touch. His breathing was rough, he moved in an occasional spasm, and was obviously asleep. The Explorer hesitated and decided not to wake him. It would serve no real purpose.

There would be no rescue, of course. That was the penalty paid for the high profits which unrestrained competition could lead to. The Merchant who opened a new planet could have a ten year monopoly if its trade, which he might hug to himself or, more likely, rent out to all comers at a stiff price. It followed that planets were searched for in secrecy and, preferably, away from the usual trade routes. In a case such as theirs, then, there was little or no chance that another ship would come within range of their subetherics except for the most improbable of coincidences. Even if they were in their ship, that is, rather than in this—this—*cage.*

The Explorer grasped the thick bars. Even if they blasted those away, as they could, they would be stuck too high in open air for leaping.

It was too bad. They had landed twice before in the scout-ship. They had established contact with the natives who were grotesquely huge, but mild and unaggressive. It was obvious that they had once owned a flourishing technology, but hadn't faced up to the consequences of such a technology. It would have been a wonderful market.

And it was a tremendous world. The Merchant, especially, had been taken aback. He had known the figures that expressed the planet's diameter, but from a distance of two light-seconds, he had stood at the visi-plate and muttered, "Unbelievable!"

"Oh, there are larger worlds," the Explorer said. It wouldn't do for an Explorer to be too easily impressed.

"Inhabited?"

"Well, no."

"Why, you could drop your planet into that large ocean and drown it."

The Explorer smiled. It was a gentle dig at his Arcturian homeland, which was smaller than most planets. He said, "Not quite."

The Merchant followed along the line of his thoughts. "And the inhabitants are large in proportion to their world?" He sounded as though the news struck him less favorably now.

"Nearly ten times our height."

"Are you sure they are friendly?"

"That is hard to say. Friendship between alien intelligences is an imponderable. They are not dangerous, I think. We've come across other groups that could not maintain equilibrium after the atomic war stage and you know the results. Introversion. Retreat. Gradual decadence and increasing gentleness."

"Even if they are such monsters?"

"The principle remains."

It was about then that the Explorer felt the heavy throbbing of the engines.

He frowned and said, "We are descending a bit too quickly."

There had been some speculation on the dangers of landing some hours before. The planetary target was a huge one for an oxygen-water world. Though it lacked the size of the uninhabitable hydrogen-ammonia planets and its low density made its surface gravity fairly normal, its gravitational forces fell off but slowly with distance. In short, its gravitational potential was high and the ship's Calculator was a run-of-the-mill model not designed to plot landing trajectories at that potential range. That meant the Pilot would have to use manual controls.

It would have been wiser to install a more high-powered model, but that would have meant a trip to some outpost of civilization; lost time; perhaps a lost secret. The Merchant demanded an immediate landing.

The Merchant felt it necessary to defend his position now. He said angrily to the Explorer, "Don't you think the Pilot knows his job? He landed you safely twice before."

Yes, thought the Explorer, in a scoutship, not in this unmaneuverable freighter. Aloud, he said nothing.

He kept his eye on the visiplate. They were descending too quickly. There was no room for doubt. Much too quickly.

The Merchant said, peevishly, "Why do you keep silence?"

"Well, then, if you wish me to speak, I would suggest that you strap on your Floater and help me prepare the Ejector."

The Pilot fought a noble fight. He was no beginner. The atmosphere, abnormally high and thick in the gravitational potential of this world whipped and burned about the ship, but to the very last it looked as though he might bring it under control despite that.

He even maintained course, following the extrapolated line to the point on the northern continent toward which they were headed. Under other circumstances, with a shade more luck, the story would eventually have been told and retold as a heroic and masterly reversal of a lost situation. But within sight of victory, tired body and tired nerves clamped a control bar with a shade too much pressure. The ship, which had almost levelled off, dipped down again.

There was no room to retrieve the final error. There was only a mile left to fall. The Pilot remained at his post to the actual landing, his only thought that of breaking the force of the crash, of maintaining the spaceworthiness of the vessel. He did not survive. With the ship bucking madly in a soupy atmosphere, few Ejectors could be mobilized and only one of them in time.

When afterwards, the Explorer lifted out of unconsciousness and rose to his feet, he had the definite feeling that but for himself and the Merchant, there were no survivors. And perhaps that was an overcalculation. His Floater had burnt out while still sufficiently distant from surface to have the fall stun him. The Merchant might have had less luck, even, than that.

He was surrounded by a world of thick, ropy stalks of grass, and in the distance were trees that reminded him vaguely of similar structures on his native Arcturian world except that their lowest branches were high above what he would consider normal tree-tops.

He called, his voice sounding basso in the thick air and the Merchant answered. The Explorer made his way toward him, thrusting violently at the coarse stalks that barred his path.

"Are you hurt?" he asked.

The Merchant grimaced, "I've sprained something. It hurts to walk."

The Explorer probed gently. "I don't think anything is broken. You'll have to walk despite the pain."

"Can't we rest first?"

"It's important to try to find the ship. If it is spaceworthy or if it can be repaired, we may live. Otherwise, we won't."

"Just a few minutes. Let me catch my breath."

The Explorer was glad enough for those few minutes. The Merchant's eyes were already closed. He allowed his to do the same.

He heard the trampling and his eyes snapped open. Never sleep on a strange planet, he told himself futilely.

The Merchant was awake too and his steady screaming was a rumble of terror.

The Explorer called, "It's only a native of this planet. It won't harm you."

But even as he spoke, the giant had swooped down and in a moment they were in its grasp being lifted closer to its monstrous ugliness.

The Merchant struggled violently and, of course, quite futilely. "Can't you talk to it?" he yelled.

The Explorer could only shake his head. "I can't reach it with the Projector. It won't be listening."

"Then blast it. Blast it down."

"We can't do that." The phrase "you fool" had almost been added. The Explorer struggled to keep his self-control. They were swallowing space as the monster moved purposefully away.

"Why not?" cried the Merchant. "You can reach your

blaster. I see it in plain sight. Don't be afraid of falling."

"It's simpler than that. If this monster is killed, you'll never trade with this planet. You'll never even leave it. You probably won't live the day out."

"Why? Why?"

"Because this is one of the young of the species. You should know what happens when a trader kills a native young, even accidentally. What's more, if this is the target-point, then we are on the estate of a powerful native. This might be one of his brood."

That was how they entered their present prison. They had carefully burnt away a portion of the thick, stiff covering and it was obvious that the height from which they were suspended was a killing one.

Now, once again, the prison-cage shuddered and lifted in an upward arc. The Merchant rolled to the lower rim and startled awake. The cover lifted and light flooded in. As was the case the time before, there were two specimens of the young. They were not very different in appearance from adults of the species, reflected the Explorer, though, of course, they were considerably smaller.

A handful of reedy green stalks was stuffed between the bars. Its odor was not unpleasant but it carried clods of soil at its ends.

The Merchant drew away and said, huskily, "What are they doing?"

The Explorer said, "Trying to feed us, I should judge. At least this seems to be the native equivalent of grass."

The cover was replaced and they were set swinging again, alone with their fodder.

IV

SLIM started at the sound of footsteps and brightened when it turned out to be only Red.

He said, "No one's around. I had my eye peeled, you bet."

Red said, "Ssh. Look. You take this stuff and stick it in the cage. I've got to scoot back to the house."

"What is it?" Slim reached reluctantly.

"Ground meat. Holy Smokes, haven't you ever seen ground meat? That's what you should've got when I sent you to the house instead of coming back with that stupid grass."

Slim was hurt. "How'd I know they don't eat grass. Besides, ground meat doesn't come loose like that. It comes in cellophane and it isn't that color."

"Sure—in the city. Out here we grind our own and it's always this color till its cooked."

"You mean it isn't cooked?" Slim drew away quickly.

Red looked disgusted. "Do you think animals eat *cooked* food. Come on, take it. It won't hurt you. I tell you there isn't much time."

"Why? What's doing back at the house?"

"I don't know. Dad and your father are walking around. I think maybe they're looking for me. Maybe the cook told them I took the meat. Anyway, we don't want them coming here after me."

"Didn't you ask the cook before you took this stuff."

"Who? That crab? Shouldn't wonder if she only let me have a drink of water because Dad makes her. Come on. Take it."

Slim took the large glob of meat though his skin crawled at the touch. He turned toward the barn and Red sped away in the direction from which he had come.

He slowed when he approached the two adults, took a few deep breaths to bring himself back to normal, and then carefully and nochalantly sauntered past. (They were walking in the general direction of the barn, he noticed, but not dead on.)

He said, "Hi, Dad. Hello, sir."

The Industrialist said, "Just a moment, Red. I have a question to ask you?"

Red turned a carefully blank face to his father. "Yes, Dad?"

"Mother tells me you were out early this morning."

"Not real early, Dad. Just a little before breakfast."

"She said you told her it was because you had been awakened during the night and didn't go back to sleep."

Red waited before answering. Should he have told Mom that?

Then he said, "Yes, sir."

"What was it that awakened you?"

Red saw no harm in it. He said, "I don't know, Dad. It sounded like thunder, sort of, and like a collision, sort of."

"Could you tell where it came from?"

"It *sounded* like it was out by the hill." That was truthful, and useful as well, since the direction was almost opposite that in which the barn lay.

The Industrialist looked at his guest. "I suppose it would do no harm to walk toward the hill."

The Astronomer said, "I am ready."

Red watched them walk away and when he turned he saw Slim peering cautiously out from among the briars of a hedge.

Red waved at him. "Come on."

Slim stepped out and approached. "Did they say anything about the meat?"

"No. I guess they don't know about that. They went down to the hill."

"What for?"

"Search me. They kept asking about the noise I heard. Listen, did the animals eat the meat?"

"Well," said Slim, cautiously, "they were sort of *looking* at it and smelling it or something."

"Okay," Red said, "I guess they'll eat it. Holy Smokes, they've got to eat *something*. Let's walk along toward the hill and see what Dad and your father are going to do."

"What about the animals?"

"They'll be all right. A fellow can't spend all his time on them. Did you give them water?"

"Sure. They drank that."

"See. Come on. We'll look at them after lunch. I tell you what. We'll bring them fruit. Anything'll eat fruit."

Together they trotted up the rise, Red, as usual, in the lead.

V

THE Astronomer said, "You think the noise was their ship landing?"

"Don't you think it could be?"

"If it were, they may all be dead."

"Perhaps not." The Industrialist frowned.

"If they have landed, and are still alive, where are they?"

"Think about that for a while." He was still frowning.

The Astronomer said, "I don't understand you."

"They may not be friendly."

"Oh, no. I've spoken with them. They've—"

"You've spoken with them. Call that reconnaissance. What would their next step be? Invasion?"

"But they only have one ship, sir."

"You know that only because they say so. They might have a fleet."

"I've told you about their size. They—"

"Their size would not matter, if they have handweapons that may well be superior to our artillery."

"That is not what I meant."

"I had this partly in mind from the first." The Industrialist went on. "It is for that reason I agreed to see them after I received your letter. Not to agree to an unsettling and impossible trade, but to judge their real purposes. I did not count on their evading the meeting."

He sighed. "I suppose it isn't our fault. You are right in one thing, at any rate. The world has been at peace too long. We are losing a healthy sense of suspicion."

The Astronomer's mild voice rose to an unusual pitch and he said, "I *will* speak. I tell you that there is no reason to suppose they can possibly be hostile. They are small, yes, but that is only important because it is a reflection of the fact that their native worlds are small. Our world has what is for them a normal gravity, but because of our much higher gravitational potential, our atmosphere is too dense to support them comfortably over sustained periods. For a similar reason the use of the world as a base for interstellar travel, except for trade in certain items, is uneconomical. And there are important differences in chemistry of life due to the basic differences in soils. They couldn't eat our food or we theirs."

"Surely all this can be overcome. They can bring their own food, build domed stations of lowered air pressure, devise specially designed ships."

"They can. And how glibly you can describe feats that are easy to a race in its youth. It is simply that they don't have to do any of that. There are millions of worlds suitable for them in the Galaxy. They don't need this one which isn't."

"How do you know? All this is their information again."

"This I was able to check independently. I am an astronomer, after all."

"That is true. Let me hear what you have to say then, while we walk."

"Then, sir, consider that for a long time our astronomers have believed that two general classes of planetary bodies existed. First, the planets which formed at distances far enough from their stellar nucleus to become cool enough to capture hydrogen. These would be large planets rich in hydrogen, ammonia and methane. We have examples of these in the giant outer planets. The second class would include those planets formed so near the stellar center that the high temperature would make it impossible to capture much hydrogen. These would be smaller planets, comparatively poorer in hydrogen and richer in oxygen. We know that type very well since we live on one. Ours is the only solar system we know in detail, however, and it has been reasonable for us to assume that these were the *only* two planetary classes."

"I take it then that there is another."

"Yes. There is a super-dense class, still smaller, poorer in hydrogen, then the inner planets of the solar system. The ratio of occurrence of hydrogen-ammonia planets and these super-dense water-oxygen worlds of theirs over the entire Galaxy—and remember that they have actually conducted a survey of significant sample volumes of the Galaxy which we, without interstellar travel, cannot do—is about 3 to 1. This leaves them seven million superdense worlds for exploration and colonization."

The Industrialist looked at the blue sky and the green-covered trees among which they were making their way. He said, "And worlds like ours?"

The Astronomer said, softly, "Ours is the first solar system they have found which contains them. Apparently the development of our solar system was unique and did not follow the ordinary rules."

The Industrialist considered that. "What it amounts to is that these creatures from space are asteroid-dwellers."

"No, no. The asteroids are something else again. They occur, I was told, in one out of eight stellar systems, but they're completely different from what we've been discussing."

"And how does your being an astronomer change the fact that you are still only quoting their unsupported statements?"

"But they did not restrict themselves to bald items of information. They presented me with a theory of stellar evolution which I had to accept and which is more nearly valid than anything our own astronomy has ever been able to devise, if we except possible lost theories dating from Beforethewars. Mind you, their theory had a rigidly mathematical development and it predicted just such a Galaxy as they describe. So you see, they have all the worlds they wish. They are not land-hungry. Certainly not for our land."

"Reason would say so, if what you say is true. But creatures may be intelligent and not reasonable. Our forefathers were presumably intelligent, yet they were certainly not reasonable. Was it reasonable to destroy almost all their tremendous civilization in atomic warfare over causes our historians can no longer accurately determine?" The Industrialist brooded over it. "From the dropping of the first atom bomb over those islands—I forget the ancient name—there was only one end in sight, and in plain sight. Yet events were allowed to proceed to that end."

He looked up, said briskly, "Well, where are we? I wonder if we are not on a fool's errand after all."

But the Astronomer was a little in advance and his voice came thickly. "No fool's errand, sir. Look there."

VI

RED and Slim had trailed their elders with the experience of youth, aided by the absorption and anxiety of their fathers. Their view of the final object of the search was somewhat obscured by the underbrush behind which they remained.

Red said, "Holy Smokes. Look at that. It's all shiny silver or something."

But it was Slim who was really excited. He caught at the other. "I know what this is. It's a space-ship. That must be why my father came here. He's one of the biggest astronomers in the world and your father would have to call him if a spaceship landed on his estate."

"What are you talking about? Dad didn't even know that thing was there. He only came here because I told him I heard the thunder from here. Besides, there isn't any such thing as a spaceship."

"Sure, there is. Look at it. See those round things. They are ports. And you can see the rocket tubes."

"How do you know so much?"

Slim was flushed. He said, "I read about them. My father has books about them. Old books. From Beforethewars."

"Huh. Now I know you're making it up. Books from Beforethewars!"

"My father *has* to have them. He teaches at the University. It's his job."

His voice had risen and Red had to pull at him. "You want them to hear us?" he whispered indignantly.

"Well, it is, too, a spaceship."

"Look here, Slim, you mean that's a ship from another world."

"It's *got* to be. Look at my father going round and round it. He wouldn't be so interested if it was anything else."

"Other worlds! Where are there other worlds?"

"Everywhere. How about the planets? They're worlds just like ours, some of them. And other stars probably have planets. There's probably zillions of planets."

Red felt outweighed and outnumbered. He muttered, "You're crazy!"

"All right, then. I'll show you."

"Hey! Where are you going?"

"Down there. I'm going to ask my father. I suppose you'll believe it if *he* tells you. I suppose you'll believe a Professor of Astronomy knows what—"

He had scrambled upright.

Red said, "Hey. You don't want them to see us. We're not supposed to be here. Do you want them to start asking questions and find out about our animals?"

"I don't care. You said I was crazy."

"Snitcher! You promised you wouldn't tell."

"I'm *not* going to tell. But if they find out themselves, it's your fault, for starting an argument and saying I was crazy."

"I take it back, then," grumbled Red.

"Well, all right. You better."

In a way, Slim was disappointed. He wanted to see the space-ship at closer quarters. Still, he could not break his vow of secrecy even in spirit without at least the excuse of personal insult.

Red said, "It's awfully small for a space-ship."

"Sure, because it's probably a scout-ship."

"I'll bet Dad couldn't even get into the old thing."

So much Slim realized to be true. It was a weak point in his argument and he made no answer. His interest was absorbed by the adults.

Red rose to his feet; an elaborate attitude of boredom all about him. "Well, I guess we better be going. There's business to do and I can't spend all day here looking at some old space-ship or whatever it is. We've got to take care of the animals if we're going to be circus-folks. That's the first rule with circus-folks. They've got to take care of the animals. And," he finished virtuously, "that's what I aim to do, anyway."

Slim said, "What for, Red.

They've got plenty of meat. Let's watch."

"There's no fun in watching. Besides Dad and your father are going away and I guess it's about lunch time."

Red became argumentative. "Look, Slim, we can't start acting suspicious or they're going to start investigating. Holy Smokes, don't you ever read any detective stories? When you're trying to work a big deal without being caught, it's practically the main thing to keep on acting just like always. Then they don't suspect anything. That's the first law—"

"Oh, all right."

Slim rose resentfully. At the moment, the circus appeared to him a rather tawdry and shoddy substitute for the glories of astronomy, and he wondered how he had come to fall in with Red's silly scheme.

Down the slope they went, Slim, as usual, in the rear.

VII

THE Industrialist said, "It's the workmanship that gets me. I never saw such construction."

"What good is it now?" said the Astronomer, bitterly. "There's nothing left. There'll be no second landing. This ship detected life on our planet through accident. Other exploring parties would come no closer than necessary to establish the fact that there were no super-dense worlds existing in our solar system."

"Well, there's no quarreling with a crash landing."

"The ship hardly seems damaged. If only some had survived, the ship might have been repaired."

"If they had survived, there would be no trade in any case. They're too different. Too disturbing. In any case—it's over."

They entered the house and the Industrialist greeted his wife calmly. "Lunch about ready, dear."

"I'm afraid not. You see—" She looked hesitantly at the Astronomer.

"Is anything wrong?" asked the Industrialist. "Why not tell me? I'm sure our guest won't mind a little family discussion."

"Pray don't pay any attention whatever to me," muttered the Astronomer. He moved miserably to the other end of the living room.

The woman said, in low, hurried tones, "Really, dear, cook's that upset. I've been soothing her for hours and honestly, I don't know why Red should have done it."

"Done what?" The Industrialist was more amused than otherwise. It had taken the united efforts of himself and his son months to argue his wife into using the name "Red" rather than the perfectly ridiculous (viewed youngster fashion) name which was his real one.

She said, "He's taken most of the chopped meat."

"He's eaten it?"

"Well, I hope not. It was raw."

"Then what would he want it for?"

"I haven't the slightest idea. I haven't seen him since breakfast. Meanwhile cook's just furious. She caught him vanishing out the kitchen door and there was the bowl of chopped meat just about empty and she was going to use it for lunch. Well, you know cook. She had to change the lunch menu and that means she won't be worth living with for a week. You'll just have to speak to Red, dear, and make him promise not to do things in the kitchen any more. And it wouldn't hurt to have him apologize to cook."

"Oh, come. She works for us. If we don't complain about a change in lunch menu, why should she?"

"Because she's the one who has double-work made for her, and she's talking about quitting. Good cooks aren't easy to get. Do you remember the one before her?"

It was a strong argument.

The Industrialist looked about vaguely. He said, "I suppose you're right. He isn't here, I suppose. When he comes in, I'll talk to him."

"You'd better start. Here he comes."

Red walked into the house and said cheerfully, "Time for lunch, I guess." He looked from one parent to the other in quick speculation at their fixed stares and said, "Got to clean up first, though," and made for the other door.

The Industrialist said, "One moment, son."

"Sir?"

"Where's your little friend?"

Red said, carelessly, "He's around somewhere. We were just sort of walking and I looked around and he wasn't there." This was perfectly true, and Red felt on safe ground. "I told him it was lunch time. I said, 'I suppose it's about lunch time.' I said, 'We got to be getting back to the house.' And he said, 'Yes.' And I just went on and then when I was about at the creek I looked around and—"

The Astronomer interrupted the voluble story, looking up from a magazine he had been sightlessly rummaging through. "I wouldn't worry about my youngster. He is quite self-reliant. Don't wait lunch for him."

"Lunch isn't ready in any case, Doctor." The Industrialist turned once more to his son. "And talking about that, son, the reason for it is that something happened to the ingredients. Do you have anything to say?"

"Sir?"

"I hate to feel that I have to explain myself more fully. Why did you take the chopped meat?"

"The chopped meat?"

"The chopped meat." He waited patiently.

Red said, "Well, I was sort of—"

"Hungry?" prompted his father. "For raw meat?"

"No, sir. I just sort of needed it."

"For what exactly?"

Red looked miserable and remained silent.

The Astronomer broke in again. "If you don't mind my putting in a few words—You'll remember that just after breakfast my son came in to ask what animals ate."

"Oh, you're right. How stupid of me to forget. Look here, Red, did you take it for an animal pet you've got?"

Red recovered indignant breath. He said, "You mean Slim came in here and said I had an animal? He came in here and said that? He said I had an animal?"

"No, he didn't. He simply asked what animals ate. That's all. Now if he promised he wouldn't tell on you, he didn't. It's your own foolishness in trying to take something without permission that gave you away. That happened to be stealing. Now have you an animal? I ask you a direct question."

"Yes, sir." It was a whisper so low as hardly to be heard.

"All right, you'll have to get rid of it. Do you understand?"

Red's mother intervened. "Do you mean to say you're keeping a meat-eating animal, Red? It might bite you and give you blood-poison."

"They're only small ones," quavered Red. "They hardly budge if you touch them."

"They? How many do you have?"

"Two."

"Where are they?"

The Industrialist touched her arm. "Don't chivvy the child any further," he said, in a low voice. "If he says he'll get rid of them, he will, and that's punishment enough."

He dismissed the matter from his mind.

VIII

LUNCH was half over when Slim dashed into the dining room. For a moment, he stood abashed, and then he said in what was almost hysteria, "I've got to speak to Red. I've got to say something."

Red looked up in fright, but the Astronomer said, "I don't think, son, you're being very polite. You've kept lunch waiting."

"I'm sorry, Father."

"Oh, don't rate the lad," said the Industrialist's wife. "He can speak to Red if he wants to, and there was no damage done to the lunch."

"I've got to speak to Red alone," Slim insisted.

"Now that's enough," said the Astronomer with a kind of gentleness that was obviously manufactured for the benefit of strangers and which had beneath it an easily-recognized edge. "Take your seat."

Slim did so, but he ate only when someone looked directly upon him. Even then he was not very successful.

Red caught his eyes. He made soundless words, "Did the animals get loose?"

Slim shook his head slightly. He whispered, "No, it's—"

The Astronomer looked at him hard and Slim faltered to a stop.

With lunch over, Red slipped out of the room, with a microscopic motion at Slim to follow.

They walked in silence to the creek.

Then Red turned fiercely upon his companion. "Look here, what's the idea of telling my Dad we were feeding animals?"

Slim said, "I didn't. I asked what you feed animals. That's not the same as saying we were doing it. Besides, it's something else, Red."

But Red had not used up his grievances. "And where did you go anyway? I thought you were coming to the house. They acted like it was my fault you weren't there."

"But I'm trying to tell you about that, if you'd only shut *up* a second and let me talk. You don't give a fellow a chance."

"Well, go on and tell me if you've got so much to say."

"I'm *trying* to. I went back to the space-ship. The folks weren't there anymore and I wanted to see what it was like."

"It isn't a space-ship," said Red, sullenly. He had nothing to lose.

"It is, too. I looked inside. You could look through the ports and I looked inside and they were *dead.*" He looked sick. "They were dead."

"*Who* were dead."

Slim screeched, "Animals! like *our* animals! Only they *aren't* animals. They're people-things from other planets."

For a moment Red might have been turned to stone. It didn't occur to him to disbelieve Slim at this point. Slim looked too genuinely the bearer of just such tidings. He said, finally, "Oh, my."

"Well, what are we going to do? Golly, will we get a whopping if they find out?" He was shivering.

"We better turn them loose," said Red.

"They'll tell on us."

"They can't talk our language. Not if they're from another planet."

"Yes, they can. Because I remember my father talking about some stuff like that to my mother when he didn't know I was in the room. He was talking about visitors who could talk with the mind. Telepathery or something. I thought he was making it up."

"Well, Holy Smokes. I mean—Holy Smokes." Red looked up. "I tell you. My Dad said to get rid of them. Let's sort of bury them somewhere or throw them in the creek."

"He *told* you to do that."

"He made me say I had animals and then he said, 'Get rid of them.' I got to do what he says. Holy Smokes, he's my Dad."

Some of the panic left Slim's heart. It was a thoroughly legalistic way out. "Well, let's do it right now, then, before they find out. Oh, golly, if they find out, will we be in trouble!"

They broke into a run toward the barn, unspeakable visions in their minds.

IX

IT WAS different, looking at them as though they were "people." As animals, they had been interesting; as "people," horrible. Their eyes, which were neutral little objects before, now seemed to watch them with active malevolence.

"They're making noises," said Slim, in a whisper which was barely audible.

"I guess they're talking or something," said Red. Funny that those noises which they had heard before had not had significance earlier. He was making no move toward them. Neither was Slim.

The canvas was off but they were just watching. The ground meat, Slim noticed, hadn't been touched.

Slim said, "Aren't you going to do something?"

"Aren't you?"

"You found them."

"It's your turn, now."

"No, it isn't. You found them. It's your fault, the whole thing. I was watching."

"You joined in, Slim. You know you did."

"I don't care. You found them and that's what I'll say when they come here looking for us."

Red said, "All right for you." But the thought of the consequences inspired him anyway, and he reached for the cage door.

Slim said, "Wait!"

Red was glad to. He said, "Now what's biting you?"

"One of them's got something on him that looks like it might be iron or something."

"Where?"

"Right there. I saw it before but I thought it was just part of him. But if he's 'people,' maybe it's a disintegrator gun."

"What's that?"

"I read about it in the books from Beforethewars. Mostly people with spaceships have disintegrator guns. They point them at you and you get disintegratored."

"They didn't point it at us till now," pointed out Red with his heart not quite in it.

"I don't care. I'm not hanging around here and getting disintegratored. I'm getting my father."

"Cowardy-cat. Yellow cowardy-cat."

"I don't care. You can call all the names you want, but if you bother them now you'll get disintegratored. You wait and see, and it'll be all your fault."

He made for the narrow spiral stairs that led to the main floor of the barn, stopped at its head, then backed away.

Red's mother was moving up, panting a little with the exertion and smiling a tight smile for the benefit of Slim in his capacity as guest.

"Red! You, Red! Are you up there? Now don't try to hide. I know this is where you're keeping them. Cook saw where you ran with the meat."

Red quavered, "Hello, ma!"

"Now show me those nasty animals? I'm going to see to it that you get rid of them right away."

It was over! And despite

the imminent corporal punishment, Red felt something like a load fall from him. At least the decision was out of his hands.

"Right there, ma. I didn't do anything to them, ma. I didn't know. They just looked like little animals and I thought you'd let me keep them, ma. I wouldn't have taken the meat only they wouldn't eat grass or leaves and we couldn't find good nuts or berries and cook never lets me have anything or I would have asked her and I didn't know it was for lunch and—"

He was speaking on the sheer momentum of terror and did not realize that his mother did not hear him but, with eyes frozen and popping at the cage, was screaming in thin, piercing tones.

X

THE Astronomer was saying, "A quiet burial is all we can do. There is no point in any publicity now," when they heard the screams.

She had not entirely recovered by the time she reached them, running and running. It was minutes before her husband could extract sense from her.

She was saying, finally, "I tell you they're in the barn. I don't know what they are. No, no—"

She barred the Industrialist's quick movement in that direction. She said, "Don't *you* go. Send one of the hands with a shotgun. I tell you I never saw anything like it. Little horrible beasts with—with—I can't describe it. To think that Red was touching them and trying to feed them. He was *holding* them, and feeding them meat."

Red began, "I only—"

And Slim said, "It was not—"

The Industrialist said, quickly, "Now you boys have done enough harm today. March! Into the house! And not a word; not one word! I'm not interested in anything you have to say. After this is all over, I'll hear you out and as for you, Red, I'll see that you're properly punished."

He turned to his wife, "Now whatever the animals are, we'll have them killed." He added quietly once the youngsters were out of hearing, "Come, come. The children aren't hurt and, after all, they haven't done anything really terrible. They've just found a new pet."

The Astronomer spoke with difficulty. "Pardon me, ma'am, but can you describe these animals?"

She shook her head. She was quite beyond words.

"Can you just tell me if they—"

"I'm sorry," said the Industrialist, apologetically, "but I think I had better take care of her. Will you excuse me?"

"A moment. Please. One moment. She said she had never seen such animals before. Surely it is not usual to find animals that are completely unique on an estate such as this."

"I'm sorry. Let's not discuss that now."

"Except that unique animals might have landed during the night."

The Industrialist stepped away from his wife. "What are you implying?"

"I think we had better go to the barn, sir!"

The Industrialist stared a moment, turned and suddenly and quite uncharacteristically began running. The Astronomer followed and the woman's wail rose unheeded behind them.

XI

THE Industrialist stared, looked at the Astronomer, turned to stare again.

"Those?"

"Those," said the Astronomer. "I have no doubt we appear strange and repulsive to them."

"What do they say?"

"Why, that they are uncomfortable and tired and even a little sick, but that they are not seriously damaged, and that the youngsters treated them well."

"Treated them well! Scooping them up, keeping them in a cage, giving them grass and raw meat to eat? Tell me how to speak to them."

"It may take a little time. Think *at* them. Try to listen. It will come to you, but perhaps not right away."

The Industrialist tried. He grimaced with the effort of it, thinking over and over again, "The youngsters were ignorant of your identity."

And the thought was suddenly in his mind: "We were quite aware of it and because we knew they meant well by us according to their own view of the matter, we did not attempt to attack them."

"Attack them?" thought the Industrialist, and said it aloud in his concentration.

"Why, yes," came the answering thought. "We are armed."

One of the revolting little creatures in the cage lifted a metal object and there was a sudden hole in the top of the cage and another in the roof of the barn, each hole rimmed with charred wood.

"We hope," the creatures thought, "it will not be too difficult to make repairs."

The Industrialist found it impossible to organize himself to the point of directed thought. He turned to the Astronomer. "And with that weapon in their possession they let themselves be handled and caged? I don't understand it."

But the calm thought came, "We would not harm the young of an intelligent species."

XII

IT WAS twilight. The Industrialist had entirely missed the evening meal and remained unaware of the fact.

He said, "Do you really think the ship will fly?"

"If they say so," said the Astronomer, "I'm sure it will. They'll be back, I hope, before too long."

"And when they do," said the Industrialist, energetically, "I will keep my part of the agreement. What is more I will move sky and earth to have the world accept them. I was entirely wrong, Doctor. Creatures that would refuse to harm children under such provocation as they received, are admirable. But you know—I almost hate to say this—"

"Say what?"

"The kids. Yours and mine. I'm almost proud of them. Imagine seizing these creatures, feeding them or trying to, and keeping them hidden. The amazing gall of it. Red told me it was his idea to get a job in a circus on the strength of them. Imagine!"

The Astronomer said, "Youth!"

XIII

THE Merchant said, "Will we be taking off soon?"

"Half an hour," said the Explorer.

It was going to be a lonely trip back. All the remaining seventeen of the crew were dead and their ashes were to be left on a strange planet. Back they would go with a limping ship and the burden of the controls entirely on himself.

The Merchant said, "It was a good business stroke, not harming the young ones. We will get very good terms; *very* good terms."

The Explorer thought: Business!

The Merchant then said,

"They've lined up to see us off. All of them. You don't think they're too close, do you? It would be bad to burn any of them with the rocket blast at this stage of the game."

"They're safe."

"Horrible looking things, aren't they?"

"Pleasant enough, inside. Their thoughts are perfectly friendly."

"You wouldn't believe it of them. That immature one, the one that first picked us up—"

"They call him Red," provided the explorer.

"That's a queer name for a monster. Makes me laugh. He actually feels *bad* that we're leaving. Only I can't make out exactly why. The nearest I can come to it is something about a lost opportunity with some organization or other that I can't quite interpret."

"A circus," said the Explorer, briefly.

"What? Why, the impertinent monstrosity."

"Why not? What would you have done if you had found *him* wandering on *your* native world; found him sleeping on a field on Earth, red tentacles, six legs, pseudopods and all?"

XIV

RED watched the ship leave. His red tentacles, which gave him his nickname, quivered their regret at lost opportunity to the very last, and the eyes at their tips filled with drifting yellowish crystals that were the equivalent of Earthly tears.

It's an encouraging sign to see the comic strips and the hard-cover book originals finally being done by someone who really knows science fiction. Jack Williamson has recently gotten into both fields. His new comic strip, BEYOND MARS, has just started, and looks good. And Simon & Schuster have just brought out a hitherto-unpublished book—DRAGON'S ISLAND (246 pp., $2.50). It's the story of a group of created supermen, and one man who must track them down. The solution involves an improbable switch of character and social thinking that seems hard to swallow, but Williamson's craftsmanship makes it a lively and suspenseful story. We hope to see more of these originals, and we suggest that you put this book on the top of your purchase list.

BOOK REVIEWS

SCIENCE—Fact and Fiction

by GEORGE O. SMITH

AS OF THIS MOMENT there is a clean slate, with no tradition to follow and no past mistakes to soft pedal here. I have an idea or two to offer, but only time will tell whether these ideas will become traditions or mistakes. For instance, I have the notion that the regular reader of science fiction is often interested in science non-fiction. Therefore, I shall attempt to include books which are of general interest to science fiction readers but which might be omitted if this were to be a straight science fiction review column. I guarantee to avoid textbooks!

I also have the notion that books should be panned when they merit it, and that there is no longer any excuse for cries of joy just because science fiction comes in hard covers. Happily, one announcement which should be received with such cries of joy is:

SLAN by A. E. an Vogt, $2.50, Simon and Schuster • We consider *Slan* one of the ten best science fiction tales of the past twenty years, so if you have not had your chance to read this account of a superman who must struggle against all mankind, as well as his own superkind, you have a real treat coming. There have been a few revisions made since the tale first appeared in *Astounding Science Fiction* in 1940 which enhance the plot.

TIME AND AGAIN by Clifford D. Simak, $2.50, Simon and Schuster • This is a time-paradox yarn about a man who discovers Destiny. Asher Sutton feels that dogs, cats and adroids are also entitled to Destiny, and he spends his early life fighting those who hope to prevent his writing the book he is destined to write and those who hope to coerce him into writing it their way. The future holds a frightful war between men and androids over that book. The resolution of Sutton's personal, public, mental and temporal problems makes good suspense and interest. There has been some rewriting and a slightly revised ending from the serial version (*Time Quarry, Galaxy Science Fiction*) which improve the mood of the story.

Among the current non-fiction books, one that deserves mention is A FEW BUTTONS MISSING by James T. Fisher, M.D , and Lowell S Hawley, $3.75, Lippincott • This is the autobiography of a psychiatrist who was active in the field for some fifty years before he wrote this book. It is highly recommended for its literary value, its wit and humor, and its sensible approach to a subject usually attacked from a sensational point of view. Doctor Fisher does not attempt to explain why you like to wear mashed potatoes in your hair; in fact, he is inclined to scoff at the type of individual who has a label for everything, a pigeonhole for everyone, and a six-minute cure for the ills of the human race.

We come next to the anthologies. If there is a publisher who has no anthology to offer, we cannot name him offhand. Things are getting tough for the collectors and editors of anthologies. They are starting to print tales that have been printed elsewhere not too long ago and stories that are still current newsstand merchandise.

We all have yellowed magazines on our shelves that contain stories that gave us a big bang; we know others who go into a pleasant glow when a well-loved title, situation, or tag-line is mentioned. These are the tales that should be slapped between hard covers and kept in good shape. But the present habit of anthologizing stories at the same time they appear on the newsstand is too much like attempting to predict that this particular story is going to be one of those which will withstand the Test of Time.

Another annoyance comes from the modest titles. I'm puzzled by the number of "Best" collections available.

However, none of the above objections can be aimed at THE ASTOUNDING SCIENCE FICTION ANTHOLOGY selected by John W. Campbell Jr., $3.95, Simon and Schuster • Campbell does not claim his selections are the best of anything but his own personal preference over the past twelve years. We find little quarrel with him. The table of contents is long, nicely diversified as to material, and neatly spread as to length. A few of the stories have appeared elsewhere, but to balance this there are a number of other bits that are rather hard to come by, even in their original magazine form. None seemed to be picked because they fit a hole or for some other uninteresting reason known only to editors. This anthology was selected to show the evolution of science fiction from an earlier taste to the present form, and this it does. Considering that it contains 23 stories and over 600 pages, the pounds per dollar adds up to a volume worth the price.

This cleans up the current list, with one little item of what might be called Historic Interest. Kimball Kinnison just went thataway on his Bergenholm in GRAY LENSMAN, $3.00, Fantasy Press • The author, of course, is E. E. Smith, mentioned for the benefit of fans under the age of eight who may not have heard tell.

THE EGO MACHINE

by HENRY KUTTNER

When a slightly mad robot drunk on AC, wants you to join an experiment in optimum ecology—don't do it! After all, who wants to argue like Disraeli or live like Ivan the Terrible?

I

NICHOLAS MARTIN looked up at the robot across the desk.

"I'm not going to ask what you want," he said, in a low, restrained voice. "I already know. Just go away and tell St. Cyr I approve. Tell him I think it's wonderful, putting a robot in the picture. We've had everything else by now, except the Rockettes. But clearly a quiet little play about Christmas among the Portuguese fishermen on the Florida coast *must* have a robot. Only, why not six robots? Tell him I suggest a baker's dozen. Go away."

"Was your mother's name Helena Glinska?" the robot asked.

"It was not," Martin said.

"Ah, then she must have been the Great Hairy One," the robot murmured.

Martin took his feet off the desk and sat up slowly.

"It's quite all right," the robot said hastily. "You've been chosen for an ecological experiment, that's all. But it won't hurt. Robots are perfectly normal life forms where I come from, so you needn't—"

"Shut up," Martin said. "Robot indeed, you—you bit-player! This time St. Cyr has gone too far." He began to shake slightly all over, with some repressed but strong emotion. The intercom box on the desk caught his eye, and he stabbed a finger at one of the switches. "Get me Miss Ashby! Right away!"

"I'm so sorry," the robot said apologetically. "Have I made a mistake? The threshold fluctuations in the neurons always upset my mnemonic norm when I temporalize. Isn't this a crisis-point in your life?"

Martin breathed hard, which seemed to confirm the robot's assumption.

"Exactly," it said. "The ecological imbalance approaches a peak that may destroy the life-form, unless . . . mm-m. Now either you're about to be stepped on by a mammoth, locked in an iron mask, assassinated by helots, or—is this Sanskrit I'm speaking?" He shook his gleaming head. "Perhaps I should have got off fifty years ago, but I thought—sorry. Good-bye," he added hastily as Martin raised an angry glare.

Then the robot lifted a finger to each corner of his naturally rigid mouth, and moved his fingers horizontally in opposite directions, as though sketching an apologetic smile.

"No, don't go away," Martin said. "I want you right here, where the sight of you can refuel my rage in case it's needed. I wish to God I could get mad and stay mad," he added plaintively, gazing at the telephone.

"Are you sure your mother's name wasn't Helena Glinska?" the robot asked. It pinched thumb and forefinger together between its nominal brows, somehow giving the impression of a worried frown.

"Naturally I'm sure," Martin snapped.

"You aren't married yet, then? To Anastasia Zakharina-Koshkina?"

"Not yet or ever," Martin replied succinctly. The telephone rang. He snatched it up.

"HELLO, Nick," said Erika Ashby's calm voice. "Something wrong?"

Instantly the fires of rage went out of Martin's eyes, to be replaced by a tender, rose-pink glow. For some years now he had given Erika, his very competent agent, ten percent of his take. He had also longed hopelessly to give her approximately a pound of flesh—the cardiac muscle, to put it in cold, unromantic terms. Martin did not; he put it in no terms at all, since whenever he tried to propose marriage to Erika he was taken with such fits of modesty that he could only babble o' green fields.

"Well," Erika repeated. "Something wrong?"

"Yes," Martin said, drawing a long breath. "Can St. Cyr make me marry somebody named Anastasia Zakharina-Koshkina?"

"What a wonderful memory you have," the robot put in mournfully. "Mine used to be, before I started temporalizing. But even radioactive neurons won't stand—"

"Nominally you're still entitled to life, liberty, et cetera," Erika said. "But I'm busy right now, Nick. Can't it wait till I see you?"

"When?"

"Didn't you get my message?" Erika demanded.

"Of course not," Martin said, angrily. "I've suspected for some time that all my incoming calls have to be cleared by St. Cyr. Somebody might try to smuggle in a word of hope, or possibly a file." His voice brightened. "Planning a jailbreak?"

"Oh, this is outrageous," Erika said. "Some day St. Cyr's going to go too far—"

"Not while he's got DeeDee behind him," Martin said gloomily. Summit Studios would sooner have made a film promoting atheism than offend their top box-office star, DeeDee Fleming. Even Tolliver Watt, who owned Summit lock, stock and barrel, spent wakeful nights because St. Cyr refused to let the lovely DeeDee sign a long-term contract.

"Nevertheless, Watt's no fool," Erika said. "I still think we could get him to give you a contract release if we could make him realize what a rotten investment you are. There isn't much time, though."

"Why not?"

"I told you—oh. Of course you don't know. He's leaving for Paris tomorrow morning."

Martin moaned. "Then I'm doomed," he said. "They'll pick up my option automatically next week and I'll never draw a free breath again. Erika, do something!"

"I'm going to," Erika said. "That's exactly what I want to see you about. Ah," she added suddenly, "now I understand why St. Cyr stopped my message. He was afraid. Nick, do you know what we've got to do?"

"See Watt?" Nick hazarded unhappily. "But Erika—"

"See Watt *alone*," Erika amplified.

"Not if St. Cyr can help it," Nick reminded her.

"Exactly. Naturally St. Cyr doesn't want us to talk to Watt privately. We might make him see reason. But this time, Nick, we've simply got to manage it somehow. One of us is going to talk to Watt while the other keeps St. Cyr at bay. Which do you choose?"

"Neither," Martin said promptly.

"Oh, Nick! I can't do the whole thing alone. Anybody'd think you were afraid of St. Cyr."

"I *am* afraid of St. Cyr," Martin said.

"Nonsense. What could he actually do to you?"

"He could terrorize me. He does it all the time. Erika, he says I'm indoctrinating beautifully. Doesn't it make your blood run cold? Look at all the other writers he's indoctrinated."

"I know. I saw one of them on Main Street last week, delving into garbage cans. Do you want to end up that way? Then stand up for your rights!"

"Ah," said the robot wisely, nodding. "Just as I thought. A crisis-point."

"Shut up," Martin said. "No, not you, Erika. I'm sorry."

"So am I," Erika said tartly. "For a moment I thought you'd acquired a backbone."

"If I were somebody like Hemingway—" Martin began in a miserable voice.

"Did you say Hemingway?" the robot inquired. "Is this

the Kinsey-Hemingway era? Then I must be right. You're Nicholas Martin, the next subject. Martin, Martin? Let me see—oh yes, the Disraeli type, that's it." He rubbed his forehead with a grating sound. "Oh, my poor neuron thresholds! Now I remember."

"NICK, can you hear me?" Erika's voice inquired. "I'm coming over there right away. Brace yourself. We're going to beard St. Cyr in his den and convince Watt you'll never make a good screen-writer. Now—"

"But St. Cyr won't *ever* admit that," Martin cried. "He doesn't know the meaning of the word failure. He says so. He's going to make me into a screen-writer or kill me."

"Remember what happened to Ed Cassidy?" Erika reminded him grimly. "St. Cyr didn't make him into a screen-writer."

"True. Poor old Ed," Martin said, with a shiver.

"All right, then. I'm on my way. Anything else?"

"Yes!" Martin cried, drawing a deep breath. "Yes, there is! I love you madly!"

But the words never got past his glottis. Opening and closing his mouth noiselessly, the cowardly playwright finally clenched his teeth and tried again. A faint, hopeless squeak vibrated the telephone's disk. Martin let his shoulders slump hopelessly. It was clear he could never propose to anybody, not even a harmless telephone.

"Did you say something?" Erika asked. "Well, good-bye then."

"Wait a minute," Martin said, his eyes suddenly falling once more upon the robot. Speechless on one subject only, he went on rapidly, "I forgot to tell you. Watt and the nest-fouling St. Cyr have just hired a mock-up phony robot to play in *Angelina Noel!*"

But the line was dead.

"I'm not a phony," the robot said, hurt.

Martin fell back in his chair and stared at his guest with dull, hopeless eyes. "Neither was King Kong," he remarked. "Don't start feeding me some line St. Cyr's told you to pull. I know he's trying to break my nerve. He'll probably do it, too. Look what he's done to my play already. Why Fred Waring? I don't mind Fred Waring in his proper place. There he's fine. But not in *Angelina Noel.* Not as the Portuguese captain of a fishing boat manned by his entire band, accompanied by

Dan Dailey singing *Napoli* to DeeDee Fleming in a mermaid's tail—"

Self-stunned by this recapitulation, Martin put his arms on the desk, his head in his hands, and to his horror found himself giggling. The telephone rang. Martin groped for the instrument without rising from his semi-recumbent position.

"Who?" he asked shakily. "*Who?* St. Cyr—"

A hoarse bellow came over the wire. Martin sat bolt upright, seizing the phone desperately with both hands.

"Listen!" he cried. "Will you let me finish what I'm going to say, just for once? Putting a robot in *Angelina Noel* is simply—"

"I do not hear what you say," roared a heavy voice. "Your idea stinks. Whatever it is. Be at Theater One for yesterday's rushes At once!"

"But wait—"

St. Cyr belched and hung up. Martin's strangling hands tightened briefly on the telephone. But it was no use. The real strangle-hold was the one St. Cyr had around Martin's throat, and it had been tightening now for nearly thirteen weeks. Or had it been thirteen years? Looking backward, Martin could scarcely believe that only a short time ago he had been a free man, a successful Broadway playwright, the author of the hit play *Angelina Noel.* Then had come St. Cyr. . . .

A snob at heart, the director loved getting his clutches on hit plays and name writers. Summit Studios, he had roared at Martin, would follow the original play exactly and would give Martin the final okay on the script, provided he signed a thirteen-week contract to help write the screen treatment. This had seemed too good to be true—and was.

Martin's downfall lay partly in the fine print and partly in the fact that Erika Ashby had been in the hospital with a bad attack of influenza at the time. Buried in legal verbiage was a clause that bound Martin to five years of servitude with Summit should they pick up his option. Next week they would certainly do just that, unless justice prevailed.

"I THINK I need a drink," Martin said unsteadily. "Or several." He glanced toward the robot. "I wonder if you'd mind getting me that bottle of Scotch from the bar over there."

"But I am here to conduct an experiment in optimum ecology," said the robot.

Martin closed his eyes. "Pour me a drink," he pleaded. "Please. Then put the glass in my hand, will you? It's not much to ask. After all, we're both human beings, aren't we?"

"Well, no," the robot said, placing a brimming glass in Martin's groping fingers. Martin drank. Then he opened his eyes and blinked at the tall highball glass in his hand. The robot had filled it to the brim with Scotch. Martin turned a wondering gaze on his metallic companion.

"You must do a lot of drinking yourself," he said thoughtfully. "I suppose tolerance can be built up. Go ahead. Help yourself. Take the rest of the bottle."

The robot placed the tip of a finger above each eye and slid the fingers upward, as though raising his eyebrows inquiringly.

"Go on, have a jolt," Martin urged. "Or don't you want to break bread with me, under the circumstances?"

"How can I?" the robot asked. "I'm a robot." His voice sounded somewhat wistful. "What happens?" he inquired. "Is it a lubricatory or a fueling mechanism?"

Martin glanced at his brimming glass.

"Fueling," he said tersely. "High octane. You really believe in staying in character, don't you? Why not—"

"Oh, the principle of irritation," the robot interrupted. "I see. Just like fermented mammoth's milk."

Martin choked. "Have you ever drunk fermented mammoth's milk?" he inquired.

"How could I?" the robot asked. "But I've seen it done." He drew a straight line vertically upward between his invisible eyebrows, managing to look wistful. "Of course my world is perfectly functional and functionally perfect, but I can't help finding temporalizing a fascina—" He broke off. "I'm wasting space-time. Ah. Now. Mr. Martin, would you be willing to—"

"Oh, have a drink," Martin said. "I feel hospitable. Go ahead, indulge me, will you? My pleasures are few. And I've got to go and be terrorized in a minute, anyhow. If you can't get that mask off I'll send for a straw. You can step out of character long enough for one jolt, can't you?"

"I'd like to try it," the robot said pensively. "Ever since I noticed the effect fermented mammoth's milk had on the boys, it's been on my mind, rather. Quite easy for a human, of course. Technically it's simple enough, I see now. The irritation just increases the frequency of the brain's kappa waves, as with boosted voltage, but since electrical voltage never existed in pre-robot times—"

"It did," Martin said, taking another drink. "I mean, it does. What do you call that, a mammoth?" He indicated the desk lamp.

The robot's jaw dropped.

"That?" he asked in blank amazement. "Why—why then all those telephone poles and dynamos and lighting-equipment I noticed in this era are powered by electricity!"

"What did you think they were powered by?" Martin asked coldly.

"Slaves," the robot said, examining the lamp. He switched it on, blinked, and then unscrewed the bulb. "Voltage, you say?"

"Don't be a fool," Martin said. "You're overplaying your part. I've got to get going in a minute. Do you want a jolt or don't you?"

"Well," the robot said, "I don't want to seem unsociable. This *ought* to work." So saying, he stuck his finger in the lamp-socket. There was a brief, crackling flash. The robot withdrew his finger.

"*F(t)*—" he said, and swayed slightly. Then his fingers came up and sketched a smile that seemed, somehow, to express delighted surprise.

"*Fff(t)!*" he said, and went on rather thickly, "*F(t)* integral between plus and minus infinity . . . *a-sub-n* to *e*. . . ."

Martin's eyes opened wide with shocked horror. Whether a doctor or a psychiatrist should be called in was debatable, but it was perfectly evident that this was a case for the medical profession, and the sooner the better. Perhaps the police, too. The bit-player in the robot suit was clearly as mad as a hatter. Martin poised indecisively, waiting for his lunatic guest either to drop dead or spring at his throat.

The robot appeared to be smacking his lips, with faint clicking sounds.

"Why, that's wonderful," he said. "AC, too."

"Y-you're not dead?" Martin inquired shakily.

"I'm not even alive," the robot murmured. "The way you'd understand it, that is. Ah—thanks for the jolt."

MARTIN stared at the robot with the wildest dawning of surmise.

"Why—" he gasped. "Why—*you're a robot!*"

"Certainly I'm a robot," his

guest said. "What slow minds you pre-robots had. Mine's working like lightning now." He stole a drunkard's glance at the desk-lamp. "*F(t)*—I mean, if you counted the kappa waves of my radio-atomic brain now, you'd be amazed how the frequency's increased." He paused thoughtfully. "*F(t),*" he added.

Moving quite slowly, like a man under water, Martin lifted his glass and drank whiskey. Then, cautiously, he looked up at the robot again.

"*F(t)*—" he said, paused, shuddered, and drank again. That did it. "I'm drunk," he said with an air of shaken relief. "That must be it. I was almost beginning to believe—"

"Oh, nobody believes I'm a robot at first," the robot said. "You'll notice I showed up in a movie lot, where I wouldn't arouse suspicion. I'll appear to Ivan Vasilovich in an alchemist's lab, and he'll jump to the conclusive I'm an automaton. Which, of course, I *am*. Then there's a Uighur on my list—I'll appear to him in a shaman's hut and he'll assume I'm a devil. A matter of ecologicologic."

"Then you're a devil?" Martin inquired, seizing on the only plausible solution.

"No, no, no. I'm a robot. Don't you understand anything?"

"I don't even know who I am, now," Martin said. "For all I know, I'm a faun and you're a human child. I don't think this Scotch is doing me as much good as I'd—"

"Your name is Nicholas Martin," the robot said patiently. "And mine is ENIAC."

"Eniac?"

"ENIAC," the robot corrected, capitalizing. "ENIAC Gamma the Ninety-Third."

So saying, he unslung a sack from his metallic shoulder and began to rummage out length upon length of what looked like red silk ribbon with a curious metallic lustre. After approximately a quarter-mile of it had appeared, a crystal football helmet emerged attached to its end. A gleaming red-green stone was set on each side of the helmet.

"Just over the temporal lobes, you see," the robot explained, indicating the jewels. "Now you just set it on your head, like this—"

"Oh no I don't," Martin said, withdrawing his head with the utmost rapidity. "Neither do you, my friend. What's the idea? I don't like the looks of that gimmick. I particularly don't like those two red garnets on the sides. They look like eyes."

"Those are artificial eclogite," the robot assured him. "They simply have a high dielectric constant. It's merely a matter of altering the normal thresholds of the neuron memory-circuits. All thinking is based on memory, you know. The strength of your associations—the emotional indices of your memories—channel your actions and decisions, and the ecologizer simply changes the voltage of your brain so the thresholds are altered."

"Is that all it does?" Martin asked suspiciously.

"Well, now," the robot said with a slight air of evasion. "I didn't intend to mention it, but since you ask—it also imposes the master-matrix of your character type. But since that's the prototype of your character in the first place, it will simply enable you to make the most of your potential ability, hereditary and acquired. It will make you react to your environment in the way that best assures your survival."

"Not me, it won't," Martin said firmly. "Because you aren't going to put that thing on my head."

The robot sketched a puzzled frown. "Oh," he said after a pause. "I haven't explained yet, have I? It's very simple. Would you be willing to take part in a valuable socio-cultural experiment for the benefit of all mankind?"

"No," Martin said.

"But you don't know what it is yet," the robot said plaintively. "You'll be the only one to refuse, after I've explained everything thoroughly. By the way, can you understand me all right?"

Martin laughed hollowly. "Natch," he said.

"Good," the robot said, relieved. "That may be one trouble with my memory. I had to record so many languages before I could temporalize. Sanskrit's very simple, but medieval Russian's confusing, and as for Uighur—however! The purpose of this experiment is to promote the most successful pro-survival relationship between man and his environment. Instant adaptation is what we're aiming at, and we hope to get it by minimizing the differential between individual and environment. In other words, the right reaction at the right time. Understand?"

"Of course not," Martin said. "What nonsense you talk."

"THERE are," the robot said rather wearily, "only a limited number of character matrices possible, depending first on the arrangement of the genes within the chromosomes, and later upon environmental additions. Since environments tend to repeat—like societies, you know—an organizational pattern isn't hard to lay out, along the Kaldekooz time-scale. You follow me so far?"

"By the Kaldekooz time-scale, yes," Martin said.

"I was always lucid," the robot remarked a little vainly, flourishing a swirl of red ribbon.

"Keep that thing away from me," Martin complained. "Drunk I may be, but I have no intention of sticking my neck out that far."

"Of course you'll do it," the robot said firmly. "Nobody's ever refused yet. And don't bicker with me or you'll get me confused and I'll have to take another jolt of voltage. Then there's no telling how confused I'll be. My memory gives me enough trouble when I temporalize. Time-travel always raises the synaptic delay threshold, but the trouble is it's so variable. That's why I got you mixed up with Ivan at first. But I don't visit him till after I've seen you—I'm running the test chronologically, and nineteen-fifty-two comes before fifteen-seventy, of course."

"It doesn't," Martin said, tilting the glass to his lips. "Not even in Hollywood does nineteen-fifty-two come before fifteen-seventy."

"I'm using the Kaldekooz time-scale," the robot explained. "But really only for convenience. Now do you want the ideal ecological differential or don't you? Because—" Here he flourished the red ribbon again, peered into the helmet, looked narrowly at Martin, and shook his head.

"I'm sorry," the robot said. "I'm afraid this won't work. Your head's too small. Not enough brain-room, I suppose. This helmet's for an eight and a half head, and yours is much too—"

"My head *is* eight and a half," Martin protested with dignity.

"Can't be," the robot said cunningly. "If it were, the helmet would fit, and it doesn't. Too big."

"It does fit," Martin said.

"That's the trouble with arguing with pre-robot species," ENIAC said, as to himself. "Low, brutish, unreasoning. No wonder, when their heads are so small. Now Mr.

Martin—" He spoke as though to a small, stupid, stubborn child. "Try to understand. This helmet's size eight and a half. Your head is unfortunately so very small that the helmet wouldn't fit—"

"Blast it!" cried the infuriated Martin, caution quite lost between Scotch and annoyance. "It does fit! Look here!" Recklessly he snatched the helmet and clapped it firmly on his head. "It fits perfectly!"

"I erred," the robot acknowledged, with such a gleam in his eye that Martin, suddenly conscious of his rashness, jerked the helmet from his head and dropped it on the desk. ENIAC quietly picked it up and put it back into his sack, stuffing the red ribbon in after it with rapid motions. Martin watched, baffled, until ENIAC had finished, gathered together the mouth of the sack, swung it on his shoulder again, and turned toward the door.

"Good-bye," the robot said. "And thank you."

"For what?" Martin demanded.

"For your cooperation," the robot said.

"I won't cooperate," Martin told him flatly. "It's no use. Whatever fool treatment it is you're selling, I'm not going to—"

"Oh, you've already had the ecology treatment," ENIAC replied blandly. "I'll be back tonight to renew the charge. It lasts only twelve hours."

"*What!*"

ENIAC moved his forefingers outward from the corners of his mouth, sketching a polite smile. Then he stepped through the door and closed it behind him.

Martin made a faint squealing sound, like a stuck but gagged pig.

Something was happening inside his head.

II

NICHOLAS MARTIN felt like a man suddenly thrust under an ice-cold shower. No, not cold—steaming hot. Perfumed, too. The wind that blew in from the open window bore with it a frightful stench of gasoline, sagebrush, paint, and—from the distant commissary—ham sandwiches.

"Drunk," he thought frantically. "I'm d r u n k—or crazy!" He sprang up and spun around wildly; then catching sight of a crack in the hardwood floor he tried to walk along it. "Because if I can walk a straight line," he thought, "I'm not drunk. I'm only crazy. . . ." It was not a very comforting thought.

He could walk it, all right. He could walk a far straighter line than the crack, which he saw now was microscopically jagged. He had, in fact, never felt such a sense of location and equilibrium in his life. His experiment carried him across the room to a wall-mirror, and as he straightened to look into it, suddenly all confusion settled and ceased. The violent sensory perceptions leveled off and returned to normal.

Everything was quiet. Everything was all right.

Martin met his own eyes in the mirror.

Everything was *not* all right.

He was stone cold sober. The Scotch he had drunk might as well have been spring-water. He leaned closer to the mirror, trying to stare through his own eyes into the depths of his brain. For something extremely odd was happening in there. All over his brain, tiny shutters were beginning to move, some sliding up till only a narrow crack remained, through which the beady little eyes of neurons could be seen peeping, some sliding down with faint crashes, revealing the agile, spidery forms of still other neurons scuttling for cover.

Altered thresholds, changing the yes-and-no reaction time of the memory-circuits, with their key emotional indices and associations . . . huh?

The robot!

Martin's head swung toward the closed office door. But he made no further move. The look of blank panic on his face very slowly, quite unconsciously, began to change. The robot . . . could wait.

Automatically Martin raised his hand, as though to adjust an invisible monocle. Behind him, the telephone began to ring. Martin glanced at it.

His lips curved into an insolent smile.

Flicking dust from his lapel with a suave gesture, Martin picked up the telephone. He said nothing. There was a long silence. Then a hoarse voice shouted, "Hello, hello, hello! Are you there? You, Martin!"

Martin said absolutely nothing at all.

"You keep me waiting," the voice bellowed. "Me, St. Cyr! Now jump! The rushes are . . . Martin, do you hear me?"

Martin gently laid down the receiver on the desk. He turned again toward the mirror, regarded himself critically, frowned.

"Dreary," he murmured. "Distinctly dreary. I wonder why I ever bought this necktie?"

The softly bellowing telephone distracted him. He studied the instrument briefly, then clapped his hands sharply together an inch from the mouthpiece. There was a sharp, anguished cry from the other end of the line.

"Very good," Martin murmured, turning away. "That robot has done me a considerable favor. I should have realized the possibilities sooner. After all, a super-machine, such as ENIAC, would be far cleverer than a man, who is merely an ordinary machine. Yes," he added, stepping into the hall and coming face to face with Toni LaMotta, who was currently working for Summit on loan. "*'Man is a machine, and woman—'*" Here he gave Miss LaMotta a look of such arrogant significance that she was quite startled.

"*'And woman—a toy,'*" Martin amplified, as he turned toward Theater One, where St. Cyr and destiny awaited him.

SUMMIT Studios, outdoing even MGM, always shot ten times as much footage as necessary on every scene. At the beginning of each shooting day, this confusing mass of celluloid was shown in St. Cyr's private projection theater, a small but luxurious domed room furnished with lie-back chairs and every other convenience, though no screen was visible until you looked up. Then you saw it on the ceiling.

When Martin entered, it was instantly evident that ecology took a sudden shift toward the worse. Operating on the theory that the old Nicholas Martin had come into it, the theater, which had breathed an expensive air of luxurious confidence, chilled toward him. The nap of the Persian rug shrank from his contaminating feet. The chair he stumbled against in the half-light seemed to shrug contemptuously. And the three people in the theater gave him such a look as might be turned upon one of the larger apes who had, by sheer accident, got an invitation to Buckingham Palace.

DeeDee Fleming (her real name was impossible to remember, besides having not a vowel in it) lay placidly in her chair, her feet comfortably up, her lovely hands folded, her large, liquid gaze fixed upon the screen where DeeDee Fleming, in the silvery meshes of a technicolor mermaid, swam phlegmatically through seas of pearl-colored mist.

Martin groped in the gloom for a chair. The strangest things were going on inside his brain, where tiny stiles still moved and readjusted until he no longer felt in the least like Nicholas Martin. Who did he feel like, then? What had happened?

He recalled the neurons whose beady little eyes he had fancied he saw staring brightly into, as well as out of, his own. Or had he? The memory was vivid, yet it couldn't be, of course. The answer was perfectly simple and terribly logical. ENIAC Gamma the Ninety-Third had told him, somewhat ambiguously, just what his ecological experiment involved. Martin had merely been given the optimum reactive pattern of his successful prototype, a man who had most thoroughly controlled his own environment. And ENIAC had told him the man's name, along with several confusing references to other prototypes like an Ivan (who?) and an unnamed Uighur.

The name for Martin's prototype was, of course, Disraeli, Earl of Beaconsfield. Martin had a vivid recollection of George Arliss playing the role. Clever, insolent, eccentric in dress and manner, exuberant, suave, self-controlled, with a strongly perceptive imagination. . . .

"No, no, no!" DeeDee said with a sort of calm impatience. "Be careful, Nick. Some other chair, please. I have my feet on this one."

"T-t-t-t-t," said Raoul St. Cyr, protruding his thick lips and snapping the fingers of an enormous hand as he pointed to a lowly chair against the wall. "Behind me, Martin. Sit down, sit down. Out of our way. Now! Pay attention. Study what I have done to make something great out of your foolish little play. Especially note how I have so cleverly ended the solo by building to five cumulative pratt-falls. Timing is all," he finished. "Now—SILENCE!"

For a man born in the obscure little Balkan country of Mixo-Lydia, Raoul St. Cyr had done very well for himself in Hollywood. In 1939 St. Cyr, growing alarmed at the imminence of war, departed for America, taking with him the print of an unpronounceable Mixo-Lydian film he had made, which might be translated roughly as *The Pores In the Face of the Peasant.*

With this he established his artistic reputation as a great director, though if the truth were known, it was really poverty that caused *The Pores* to be so artistically lighted, and simple drunkenness which had made most of the cast act out one of the strangest performances in film history. But critics compared *The Pores* to a ballet and praised inordinately the beauty of its leading lady, now known to the world as DeeDee Fleming.

DeeDee was so incredibly beautiful that the law of compensation would force one to expect incredible stupidity as well. One was not disappointed. DeeDee's neurons didn't know *anything.* She had heard of emotions, and under St. Cyr's bullying could imitate a few of them, but other directors had gone mad trying to get through the semantic block that kept DeeDee's mind a calm, unruffled pool possibly three inches deep. St. Cyr merely bellowed. This simple, primordial approach seemed to be the only one that made sense to Summit's greatest investment and top star.

With this whip-hand over the beautiful and brainless DeeDee, St. Cyr quickly rose to the top in Hollywood. He had undoubted talent. He could make one picture very well indeed. He had made it twenty times already, each time starring DeeDee, and each time perfecting his own feudalistic production unit. Whenever anyone disagreed with St. Cyr, he had only to threaten to go over to MGM and take the obedient DeeDee with him, for he had never allowed her to sign a long-term contract and she worked only on a picture-to-picture basis. Even Tolliver Watt knuckled under when St. Cyr voiced the threat of removing DeeDee.

"SIT DOWN, Martin," Tolliver Watt said. He was a tall, lean, hatchet-faced man who looked like a horse being starved because he was too proud to eat hay. With calm, detached omnipotence he inclined his grey-shot head a millimeter, while a faintly pained expression passed fleetingly across his face.

"Highball, please," he said.

A white-clad waiter appeared noiselessly from nowhere and glided forward with a tray. It was at this point that Martin felt the last stiles readjust in his brain, and entirely on impulse he reached out and took the frosted highball glass from the tray. Without observing this the waiter glided on and presented Watt with a gleaming salver full of nothing. Watt and the waiter regarded the tray.

Then their eyes met. There was a brief silence.

"Here," Martin said, replacing the glass. "Much too weak. Get me another, please. I'm reorienting toward a new phase, which means a different optimum," he explained to the puzzled Watt as he readjusted a chair beside the great man and dropped into it. Odd that he had never before felt at ease during rushes. Right now he felt fine. Perfectly at ease. Relaxed.

"Scotch and soda for Mr. Martin," Watt said calmly. "And another for me."

"So, so, so, now we begin," St. Cyr cried impatiently. He spoke into a hand microphone. Instantly the screen on the ceiling flickered noisily and began to unfold a series of rather ragged scenes in which a chorus of mermaids danced on their tails down the street of a little Florida fishing village.

To understand the full loathsomeness of the fate facing Nicholas Martin, it is necessary to view a St. Cyr production. It seemed to Martin that he was watching the most noisome movie ever put upon film. He was conscious that St. Cyr and Watt were stealing rather mystified glances at him. In the dark he put up two fingers and sketched a robot-like grin. Then, feeling sublimely sure of himself, he lit a cigarette and chuckled aloud.

"You laugh?" St. Cyr demanded with instant displeasure. "You do not appreciate great art? What do you know about it, eh? Are you a genius?"

"This," Martin said urbanely, "is the most noisome movie ever put on film."

In the sudden, deathly quiet which followed, Martin flicked ashes elegantly and added, "With my help, you may yet avoid becoming the laughing stock of the whole continent. Every foot of this picture must be junked. Tomorrow bright and early we will start all over, and—"

Watt said quietly, "We're quite competent to make a film out of *Angelina Noel*, Martin."

"It is artistic!" St. Cyr shouted. "And it will make money, too!"

"Bah, money!" Martin said cunningly. He flicked more ash with a lavish gesture.

"Who cares about money? Let Summit worry."

Watt leaned forward to peer searchingly at Martin in the dimness.

"Raoul," he said, glancing at St. Cyr, "I understood you were getting your—ah—your new writers whipped into shape. This doesn't sound to me as if—"

"Yes, yes, yes, yes," St. Cyr cried excitedly. "Whipped into shape, exactly! A brief delirium, eh? Martin, you feel well? You feel yourself?"

Martin laughed with quiet confidence. "Never fear," he said. "The money you spend on me is well worth what I'll bring you in prestige. I quite understand. Our confidential talks were not to be secret from Watt, of course."

"What confidential talks?" bellowed St. Cyr thickly, growing red.

"We need keep nothing from Watt, need we?" Martin went on imperturably. "You hired me for prestige, and prestige you'll get, if you can only keep your big mouth shut long enough. I'll make the name of St. Cyr glorious for you. Naturally you may lose something at the box-office, but it's well worth—"

"Pjrzqxgl!" roared St. Cyr in his native tongue, and he lumbered up from the chair, brandishing the microphone in an enormous, hairy hand.

Deftly Martin reached out and twitched it from his grasp.

"Stop the film," he ordered crisply.

It was very strange. A distant part of his mind knew that normally he would never have dared behave this way, but he felt convinced that never before in his life had he acted with complete normality. He glowed with a giddy warmth of confidence that everything he did would be right, at least while the twelve-hour treatment lasted. . . .

THE screen flickered hesitantly, then went blank.

"Turn the lights on," Martin ordered the unseen presence beyond the mike. Softly and suddenly the room glowed with illumination. And upon the visages of Watt and St. Cyr he saw a mutual dawning uneasiness begin to break.

He had just given them food for thought. But he had given them more than that. He tried to imagine what moved in the minds of the two men, below the suspicions he had just implanted. St. Cyr's was fairly obvious. The Mixo-Lydian licked his lips—no mean task—and studied Martin with uneasy little bloodshot eyes. Clearly Martin had acquired confidence from somewhere. What did it mean? What secret sin of St. Cyr's had been discovered to him, what flaw in his contract, that he dared behave so defiantly?

Tolliver Watt was a horse of another color; apparently the man had no guilty secrets; but he too looked uneasy. Martin studied the proud face and probed for inner weaknesses. Watt would be a harder nut to crack. But Martin could do it.

"That last underwater sequence," he now said, pursuing his theme. "Pure trash, you know. It'll have to come out. The whole scene must be shot from under water."

"Shut up!" St. Cyr shouted violently.

"But it must, you know," Martin went on. "Or it won't jibe with the new stuff I've written in. In fact, I'm not at all certain that the whole picture shouldn't be shot under

(Continued on next page)

COMING EVENTS

- Next issue will bring our first SPACE Special—a term we promise to use only for something unique. Conan the Cimmerian—probably the most famous swashbuckling hero of fantasy fiction—is back! This is an unpublished story, and deals with the early life of Conan. It's by Robert E. Howard, of course. You might pass the word along.

- Murray Leinster has a story of the first man to crack the speed of light—which made him a fool! *The Barrier* has the emotional punch we expect from a master story teller.

- William Tenn, another master, has a story of a tempest in a teapot—with a spaceship stirring up the tempest! Fletcher Pratt gives us a story of how a planet is conquered—but with a neat twist on who conquers whom. And there'll be other stories to round out 160 pages of the best features and fiction we can jam into one magazine.

- You'll find it on the newsstand the first of June. If it's too much trouble to look there, we'd like to remind you that a year's subscription will cost only $2—and you'll be sure not to miss your copy.

water. You know, we could use the documentary technique—"

"Raoul," Watt said suddenly, "what's this man trying to do?"

"He is trying to break his contract, of course," St. Cyr said, turning ruddy olive. "It is the bad phase all my writers go through before I get them whipped into shape. In Mixo-Lydia—"

"Are you sure he'll whip into shape?" Watt asked.

"To me this is now a personal matter," St. Cyr said, glaring at Martin. "I have spent nearly thirteen weeks on this man and I do not intend to waste my valuable time on another. I tell you he is simply trying to break his c o n t r a c t—tricks, tricks, tricks."

"Are you?" Watt asked Martin coldly.

"Not now," Martin said. "I've changed my mind. My agent insists I'd be better off away from Summit. In fact, she has the curious feeling that I and Summit would suffer by a mesalliance. But for the first time I'm not sure I agree. I begin to see possibilities, even in the tripe St. Cyr has been stuffing down the public's throat for years. Of course I can't work miracles all at once. Audiences have come to expect garbage from Summit, and they've even been conditioned to like it. But we'll begin in a small way to re-educate them with this picture. I suggest we try to symbolize the Existentialist hopelessness of it all by ending the film with a full four hundred feet of seascapes—nothing but vast, heaving stretches of ocean," he ended, on a note of complacent satisfaction.

A vast, heaving stretch of Raoul St. Cyr rose from his chair and advanced upon Martin.

"Outside, outside!" he shouted. "Back to your cell, you double-crossing vermin! I, Raoul St. Cyr, command it. Outside, before I rip you limb from limb—"

Martin spoke quickly. His voice was calm, but he knew he would have to work fast.

"You see, Watt?" he said clearly, meeting Watt's rather startled gaze. "Doesn't dare let you exchange three words with me, for fear I'll let something slip. No wonder he's trying to put me out of here —he's skating on thin ice these days."

Goaded, St. Cyr rolled forward in a ponderous lunge, but Watt interposed. It was true, of course, that the writer was probably trying to break his contract. But there were wheels within wheels here. Martin was too confident, too debonaire. Something was going on which Watt did not understand.

"All right, Raoul," he said decisively. "Relax for a minute. I said relax! We don't want Nick here suing you for assault and battery, do we? Your artistic temperament carries you away sometimes. Relax and let's hear what Nick has to say."

"Watch out for him, Tolliver!" St. Cyr cried warningly. "They're cunning, these creatures. Cunning as rats. You never know—"

Martin raised the microphone with a lordly gesture. Ignoring the director, he said commandingly into the mike, "Put me through to the commissary. The bar, please. Yes. I want to order a drink. Something very special. A—ah—a Helena Glinska—"

"HELLO," Erika Ashby's voice said from the door. "Nick, are you there? May I come in?"

The sound of her voice sent delicious chills rushing up and down Martin's spine. He swung round, mike in hand, to welcome her. But St. Cyr, pleased at this diversion, roared before he could speak.

"No, no, no, no! Go! Go at once. Whoever you are—*out!*"

Erika, looking very brisk, attractive and firm, marched into the room and cast at Martin a look of resigned patience.

Very clearly she expected to fight both her own battles and his.

"I'm on business here," she told St. Cyr coldly. "You can't part author and agent like this. Nick and I want to have a word with Mr. Watt."

"Ah, my pretty creature, sit down," Martin said in a loud, clear voice, scrambling out of his chair. "Welcome! I'm just ordering myself a drink. Will you have something?"

Erika looked at him with startled suspicion. "No, and neither will you," she said. "How many have you had already? Nick, if you're drunk at a time like this—"

"And no shilly-shallying," Martin said blandly into the mike. "I want it at once, do you hear? A Helena Glinska, yes. Perhaps you don't know it? Then listen carefully. Take the largest Napoleon you've got. If you haven't a big one, a small punch bowl will do. Fill it half full with ice-cold ale. Got that? Add three jiggers of creme de menthe—"

"Nick, are you mad?" Erika demanded, revolted.

"—and six jiggers of honey," Martin went on placidly. "Stir, don't shake. Never shake a Helena Glinska. Keep it well chilled, and—"

"Miss Ashby, we are very busy," St. Cyr broke in importantly, making shooing motions toward the door. "Not now. Sorry. You interrupt. Go at once."

"—better add six more jiggers of honey," Martin was heard to add contemplatively into the mike. "And then send it over immediately. Drop everything else, and get it here within sixty seconds. There's a bonus for you if you do. Okay? Good. See to it."

He tossed the microphone casually at St. Cyr.

Meanwhile, Erika had closed in on Tolliver Watt.

"I've just come from talking to Gloria Eden," she said, "and she's willing to do a one-picture deal with Summit *if* I okay it. But I'm not going to okay it unless you release Nick Martin from his contract, and that's flat."

Watt showed pleased surprise.

"Well, we might get together on that," he said instantly, for he was a fan of Miss Eden's and for a long time had yearned to star her in a remake of *Vanity Fair*. "Why didn't you bring her along? We could have—"

"Nonsense!" St. Cyr shouted. "Do not discuss this matter yet, Tolliver."

"She's down at Laguna," Erika explained. "Be quiet, St. Cyr! I won't—"

A knock at the door interrupted her. Martin hurried to open it and as he had expected encountered a waiter with a tray.

"Quick work," he said urbanely, accepting the huge, coldly sweating Napoleon in a bank of ice. "Beautiful, isn't it?"

St. Cyr's booming shouts from behind him drowned out whatever remark the waiter may have made as he received a bill from Martin and withdrew, looking nauseated.

"No, no, no, no," St. Cyr was roaring. "Tolliver, we can get Gloria and keep this writer too, not that he is any good, but I have spent already thirteen weeks training him in the St. Cyr approach. Leave it to me. In Mixo-Lydia we handle—"

Erika's attractive mouth was opening and shutting, her voice unheard in the uproar. St. Cyr could keep it up indefinitely, as was well known in Hollywood. Martin sighed, lifted the brimming Napoleon and sniffed delicately as he stepped backward toward his chair. When his heel touched it, he tripped with the utmost grace and savoir-faire, and very deftly emptied the Helena Glinsak, ale, honey, creme de menthe, ice and all, over St. Cyr's capacious front.

St. Cyr's bellow broke the microphone.

MARTIN had composed his invention carefully. The nauseous brew combined the maximum elements of wetness, coldness, stickiness and pungency.

The drenched St. Cyr, shuddering violently as the icy beverage deluged his legs, snatched out his handkerchief and mopped in vain. The handkerchief merely stuck to his trousers, glued there by twelve jiggers of honey. He reeked of peppermint.

"I suggest we adjourn to the commissary," Martin said fastidiously. "In some private booth we can go on with this discussion away from the—the rather overpowering smell of peppermint."

"In Mixo-Lydia," St. Cyr gasped, sloshing in his shoes as he turned toward Martin, "in Mixo-Lydia we throw to the dogs—we boil in oil—we—"

"And next time," Martin said, "please don't joggle my elbow when I'm holding a Helena Glinska. It's most annoying."

St. Cyr drew a mighty breath, rose to his full height—and then subsided. St. Cyr at the moment looked like a Keystone Kop after the chase sequence, and knew it. Even if he killed Martin now, the element of classic tragedy would be lacking. He would appear in the untenable position of Hamlet murdering his uncle with custard pies.

"Do nothing until I return!" he commanded, and with a final glare at Martin plunged moistly out of the theater.

The door crashed shut behind him. There was silence for a moment except for the soft music from the overhead screen which DeeDee had caused to be turned on again, so that she might watch her own lovely form flicker in dimmed images through pastel waves, while she sang a duet with Dan Dailey about sailors, mermaids and her home in far Atlantis.

"And now," said Martin, turning with quiet authority to Watt, who was regarding him with a baffled expression, "I want a word with you."

"I can't discuss your contract till Raoul gets back," Watt said quickly.

"Nonsense," Martin said in a firm voice. "Why should St. Cyr dictate your decisions? Without you, he couldn't turn out a box-office success if he had to. No, be quiet, Erika. I'm handling this, my pretty creature."

Watt rose to his feet. "Sorry, I can't discuss it," he said. "St. Cyr pictures make money, and you're an inexperien—"

"That's why I see the true situation so clearly," Martin said. "The trouble with you is you draw a line between artistic genius and financial genius. To you, it's merely routine when you work with the plastic medium of human minds, shaping them into an Ideal Audience. You are an ecological genius, Tolliver Watt! The true artist controls his environment, and gradually you, with a master's consummate skill, shape that great mass of living, breathing humanity into a perfect audience. . . ."

"Sorry," Watt said, but not bruskly. "I really have no time—ah—"

"Your genius has gone long enough unrecognized," Martin said hastily, letting admiration ring in his golden voice. "You assume that St. Cyr is your equal. You give him your own credit titles. Yet in your own mind you must have known that half the credit for his pictures is yours. Was Phidias non-commercial? Was Michaelangelo? Commercialism is simply a label for functionalism, and all great artists produce functional art. The trivial details of Rubens' masterpieces were filled in by assistants, were they not? But Rubens got the credit, not his hirelings. The proof of the pudding's obvious. Why?" Cunningly gauging his listener, Martin here broke off.

"Why?" Watt asked.

"Sit down," Martin urged. "I'll tell you why. St. Cyr's pictures make money, but you're responsible for their molding into the ideal form, impressing your character-matrix upon everything and everyone at Summit Studios. . . ."

SLOWLY Watt sank into his chair. About his ears the hypnotic bursts of Disraelian rhodomontade thundered compellingly. For Martin had the man hooked. With unerring aim he had at the first try discovered Watt's weakness

—the uncomfortable feeling in a professionally arty town that money-making is a basically contemptible business. Disraeli had handled tougher problems in his day. He had swayed Parliaments.

Watt swayed, tottered—and fell. It took about ten minutes, all in all. By the end of that time, dizzy with eloquent praise of his economic ability, Watt had realized that while St. Cyr might be an artistic genius, he had no business interfering in the plans of an economic genius. Nobody told Watt what to do when economics were concerned.

"You have the broad vision that can balance all possibilities and show the right path with perfect clarity," Martin said glibly. "Very well. You wish Eden. You feel—do you not?—that I am unsuitable material. Only geniuses can change their plans with instantaneous speed. . . . When will my contract release be ready?"

"What?" said Watt, in a swimming, glorious daze. "Oh. Of course. Hm-m. Your contract release. Well, now—"

"St. Cyr would stubbornly cling to past errors until Summit goes broke," Martin pointed out. "Only a genius like Tolliver Watt strikes when the iron is hot, when he sees a chance to exchange failure for success, a Martin for an Eden."

"Hm-m," Watt said. "Yes. Very well, then." His long face grew shrewd. "Very well, you get your release—*after* I've signed Eden."

"There you put your finger on the heart of the matter," Martin approved, after a very brief moment of somewhat dashed thought. "Miss Eden is still undecided. If you left the transaction to somebody like St. Cyr, say, it would be botched. Erika, you have your car here? How quickly could you drive Tolliver Watt to Laguna? He's the only person with the skill to handle this situation."

"What situa—oh, yes. Of course, Nick. We could start right away."

"But—" Watt said.

The Disraeli-matrix swept on into oratorical periods that made the walls ring. The golden tongue played arpeggios with logic.

"I see," the dazed Watt murmured, allowing himself to be shepherded toward the door. "Yes, yes, of course. Then—suppose you drop over to my place tonight, Martin. After I get the Eden signature, I'll have your release prepared. Hm-m. Functional genius. . . ." His voice fell to a low, crooning mutter, and he moved quietly out of the door.

Martin laid a hand on Erika's arm as she followed him.

"Wait a second," he said. "Keep him away from the studio until we get the release. St. Cyr can still outshout me any time. But he's hooked. We—"

"Nick," Erika said, looking searchingly into his face. "What's happened?"

"Tell you tonight," Martin said hastily, hearing a distant bellow that might be the voice of St. Cyr approaching. "When I have time I'm going to sweep you off your feet. Did you know that I've worshipped you from afar all my life? But right now, get Watt out of the way. Hurry!"

Erika cast a glance of amazed bewilderment at him as he thrust her out of the door. Martin thought there was a certain element of pleasure in the surprise.

"WHERE is Tolliver?" The loud, annoyed roar of St. Cyr made Martin wince. The director was displeased, it appeared, because only in Costumes could a pair of trousers be found large enough to fit him. He took it as a personal affront. "What have you done with Tolliver?" he bellowed.

"Louder, please," Martin said insolently. "I can't hear you."

"DeeDee," St. Cyr shouted, whirling toward the lovely star, who hadn't stirred from her rapturous admiration of DeeDee in technicolor overhead. "Where is Tolliver?"

Martin started. He had quite forgotten DeeDee.

"You don't know, do you, DeeDee?" he prompted quickly.

"Shut up," St. Cyr snapped. "Answer me, you—" He added a brisk polysyllable in Mixo-Lydian, with the desired effect. DeeDee wrinkled her flawless brow.

"Tolliver went away, I think. I've got it mixed up with the picture. He went home to meet Nick Martin, didn't he?"

"See?" Martin interrupted, relieved. "No use expecting DeeDee to—"

"But Martin is *here!*" St. Cyr shouted. "Think, think!"

"Was the contract release in the rushes?" DeeDee asked vaguely.

"A contract release?" St. Cyr roared. "What is this? Never will I permit it, never, never, never! DeeDee, answer me—where has Watt gone?"

"He went somewhere with that agent," DeeDee said. "Or was that in the rushes too?"

"But where, where, where?"

"They went to Atlantis," DeeDee announced with an air of faint triumph.

"No!" shouted St. Cyr. "That was the *picture!* The mermaid came from Atlantis, not Watt!"

"Tolliver didn't say he was coming from Atlantis," DeeDee murmured, unruffled. "He said he was going to Atlantis. Then he was going to meet Nick Martin at his house tonight and give him his contract release."

"When?" St. Cyr demanded furiously. "Think, DeeDee? What time did—"

"DeeDee," Martin said, stepping forward with suave confidence, "you can't remember a thing, can you?" But DeeDee was too subnormal to react even to a Disraeli-matrix. She merely smiled placidly at him.

"Out of my way, you writer!" roared St. Cyr, advancing upon Martin. "You will get no contract release! You do not waste St. Cyr's time and get away with it! This I will not endure. I fix you as I fixed Ed Cassidy!"

Martin drew himself up and froze St. Cyr with an insolent smile. His hand toyed with an imaginary monocle. Golden periods were hanging at the end of his tongue. There only remained to hypnotize St. Cyr as he had hypnotized Watt. He drew a deep breath to unlease the floods of his eloquence—

And St. Cyr, also too subhuman to be impressed by urbanity, hit Martin a clout on the jaw.

It could never have happened in the British Parliament.

III

WHEN the robot walked into Martin's office that evening, he, or it, went directly to the desk, unscrewed the bulb from the lamp, pressed the switch, and stuck his finger into the socket. There was a crackling flash. ENIAC withdrew his finger and shook his metallic head violently.

"I needed that," he sighed. "I've been on the go all day, by the Kaldekooz time-scale. Paleolithic, Neolithic, Technological—I don't even know what time it is. Well, how's your ecological adjustment getting on?"

Martin rubbed his chin thoughtfully.

"Badly," he said. "Tell me, did Disraeli, as Prime Minister, ever have any dealings with a country called Mixo-Lydia?"

"I have no idea," said the robot. "Why do you ask?"

"Because my environment hauled back and took a poke at my jaw," Martin said shortly.

"Then you provoked it," ENIAC countered. "A crisis—a situation of stress—always brings a man's dominant trait to the fore, and Disraeli was dominantly courageous. Under stress, his courage became insolence. But he was intelligent enough to arrange his environment so insolence would be countered on the semantic level. Mixo-Lydia, eh? I place it vaguely, some billions of years ago, when it was inhabited by giant white apes. Or—oh, now I remember. It's an encysted medieval survival, isn't it?"

Martin nodded.

"So is this movie studio," the robot said. "Your trouble is that you've run up against somebody who's got a better optimum ecological adjustment than you have. That's it. This studio environment is just emerging from medievalism, so it can easily slip back into that plenum when an optimum medievalist exerts pressure. Such types caused the Dark Ages. Well, you'd better change your environment to a neo-technological one, where the Disraeli matrix can be successfully pro-survival. In your era, only a few archaic social-encystments like this studio are feudalistic, so go somewhere else. It takes a feudalist to match a feudalist."

"But I can't go somewhere else," Martin complained. "Not without my contract release. I was supposed to pick it up tonight, but St. Cyr found out what was happening, and he'll throw a monkey-wrench in the works if he has to knock me out again to do it. I'm due at Watt's place now, but St. Cyr's already there—"

"Spare me the trivia," the robot said, raising his hand. "As for this St. Cyr, if he's a medieval character-type, obviously he'll knuckle under only to a stronger man of his own kind."

"How would Disraeli have handled this?" Martin demanded.

"Disraeli would never have got into such a situation in the first place," the robot said unhelpfully. "The ecologizer can give you the ideal ecological differential, but only for your own type, because otherwise it wouldn't be your optimum. Disraeli would have been a failure in Russia in Ivan's time."

"Would you mind clarifying that?" Martin asked thoughtfully.

"Certainly," the robot said with great rapidity. "It all depends on the threshold-response-time of the memory-circuits in the brain, if you assume the identity of the basic chromosome-pattern. The strength of neuronic activation varies in inverse proportion to the quantative memory factor. Only actual experience could give you Disraeli's memories, but your reactivity-thresholds have been altered until perception and emotional-indices approximate the Disraeli ratio."

"Oh," Martin said. "But how would *you*, say, assert yourself against a medieval steam-shovel?"

"By plugging my demountable brain into a larger steam-shovel," ENIAC told him.

MARTIN seemed pensive. His hand rose, adjusting an invisible monocle, while a look of perceptive imagination suddenly crossed his face.

"You mentioned Russia in Ivan's time," he said. "Which Ivan would that be? Not, by any chance—?"

"Ivan the Fourth. Very well adjusted to his environment he was, too. However, enough of this chit-chat. Obviously you'll be one of the failures in our experiment, but our aim is to strike an average, so if you'll put the ecologizer on your—"

"That was Ivan the Terrible, wasn't it?" Martin interrupted. "Look here, could you impress the character-matrix of Ivan the Terrible on my brain?"

"That wouldn't help you a bit," the robot said. "Besides, it's not the purpose of the experiment. Now—"

"One moment. Disraeli can't cope with a medievalist like St. Cyr on his own level, but if I had Ivan the Terrible's reactive thresholds, I'll bet I could throw a bluff that might do the trick. Even though St. Cyr's bigger than I am, he's got a veneer of civilization . . . now wait. He trades on that. He's always dealt with people who are too civilized to use his own methods. The trick would be to call his bluff. And Ivan's the man who could do it."

"But you don't understand."

"Didn't everybody in Russia tremble with fear at Ivan's name?"

"Yes, in—"

"Very well, then," Martin said triumphantly. "You're going to impress the character-matrix of Ivan the Terrible on my mind, and then I'm going to put the bite on St. Cyr, the way Ivan would have done it. Disraeli's simply too civilized. Size is a factor, but character's more important. I don't *look* like Disraeli, but people have been reacting to me as though I were George Arliss down to the spit-curl. A good big man can always lick a good little man. But St. Cyr's never been up against a really uncivilized little man—one who'd gladly rip out an enemy's heart with his bare hands." Martin nodded briskly. "St. Cyr will back down—I've found that out. But it would take somebody like Ivan to make him stay all the way down."

"If you think I'm going to impress Ivan's matrix on you, you're wrong," the robot said.

"You couldn't be talked into it?"

"I," said ENIAC, "am a robot, semantically adjusted. Of course you couldn't talk me into it."

Perhaps not, Martin reflected, but Disraeli—hm-m. "Man is a machine." Why, Disraeli was the one person in the world ideally fitted for robot-coercion. To him, men *were* machines—and what was ENIAC?

"Let's talk this over—" Martin began, absently pushing the desk-lamp toward the robot. And then the golden tongue that had swayed empires was loosed. . . .

"You're not going to like this," the robot said dazedly, sometime later. "Ivan won't do at . . . oh, you've got me all confused. You'll have to eyeprint a—" He began to pull out of his sack the helmet and the quarter-mile of red ribbon.

"To tie up my bonny grey brain," Martin said, drunk with his own rhetoric. "Put it on my head. That's right. Ivan the Terrible, remember. I'll fix St. Cyr's Mixo-Lydian wagon."

"Differential depends on environment as much as on heredity," the robot muttered, clapping the helmet on Martin's head. "Though naturally Ivan wouldn't have had the Tsardom environment without his particular heredity, involving Helena Glinska—there!" He removed the helmet.

"But nothing's happening," Martin said. "I don't feel any different."

"It'll take a few moments. This isn't your basic character-pattern, remember, as

Disraeli's was. Enjoy yourself while you can. You'll get the Ivan-effect soon enough." He shouldered the sack and headed uncertainly for the door.

"Wait," Martin said uneasily. "Are you sure—"

"Be quiet. I forgot something—some formality—now I'm all confused. Well, I'll think of it later, or earlier, as the case may be. I'll see you in twelve hours—I hope."

The robot departed. Martin shook his head tentatively from side to side. Then he got up and followed ENIAC to the door. But there was no sign of the robot, except for a diminishing whirlwind of dust in the middle of the corridor.

Something began to happen in Martin's brain. . . .

Behind him, the telephone rang.

Martin heard himself gasp with pure terror. With a sudden, impossible, terrifying, absolute certainty he *knew* who was telephoning.

Assassins!

"YES, Mr. Martin," said Tolliver Watt's butler to the telephone. "Miss Ashby is here. She is with Mr. Watt and Mr. St. Cyr at the moment, but I will give her your message. You are detained. And she is to call for you—where?"

"The broom-closet on the second floor of the Writers' Building," Martin said in a quavering voice. "It's the only one near a telephone with a long enough cord so I could take the phone in here with me. But I'm not at all certain that I'm safe. I don't like the looks of that broom on my left."

"Sir?"

"Are you *sure* you're Tolliver Watt's butler?" Martin demanded nervously.

"Quite sure, Mr.—eh—Mr. Martin."

"I *am* Mr. Martin," cried Martin with terrified defiance. "By all the laws of God and man, Mr. Martin I am and Mr. Martin I will remain, in spite of all attempts by rebellious dogs to depose me from my rightful place."

"Yes, sir. The broom-closet, you say, sir?"

"The broom-closet. Immediately. But swear not to tell another soul, no matter how much you're threatened. I'll protect you."

"Very well, sir. Is that all?"

"Yes. Tell Miss Ashby to hurry. Hang up now. The line may be tapped. I have enemies."

There was a click. Martin replaced his own receiver and

furtively surveyed the broom-closet. He told himself that this was ridiculous. There was nothing to be afraid of, was there? True, the broom-closet's narrow walls were closing in upon him alarmingly, while the ceiling descended. . . .

Panic-stricken, Martin emerged from the closet, took a long breath, and threw back his shoulders. "N-not a thing to be afraid of," he said. "Who's afraid?" Whistling, he began to stroll down the hall toward the staircase, but midway agoraphobia overcame him, and his nerve broke.

He ducked into his own office and sweated quietly in the dark until he had mustered up enough courage to turn on a lamp.

The Encyclopedia Britannica, in its glass-fronted cabinet, caught his eye. With noiseless haste, Martin secured *ITALY* to *LORD* and opened the volume at his desk. Something, obviously, was very, very wrong. The robot had said that Martin wasn't going to like being Ivan the Terrible, come to think of it. But was Martin wearing Ivan's character-matrix? Perhaps he'd got somebody else's matrix by mistake—that of some arrant coward. Or maybe the Mad Tsar of Russia had really been called Ivan the Terrified. Martin flipped the rustling pages nervously. Ivan, Ivan—here it was.

Son of Helena Glinska . . . married Anastasia Zakharina-Koshkina . . . private life unspeakably abominable . . . memory astonishing, energy indefatigable, ungovernable fury—great natural ability, political foresight, anticipated the ideals of Peter the Great— Martin shook his head.

Then he caught his breath at the next line.

Ivan had lived in an atmosphere of apprehension, imagining that every man's hand was against him.

"Just like me," Martin murmured. "But—but there was more to Ivan than just cowardice. I don't understand."

"Differential," the robot had said, "depends on environment as much as on heredity. Though naturally Ivan wouldn't have had the Tsardom environment without his particular heredity."

Martin sucked in his breath sharply. Environment does make a difference. No doubt Ivan IV had been a fearful coward, but heredity plus environment had given Ivan the one great weapon that had enabled him to keep his cowardice a recessive trait.

Ivan the Terrible had been Tsar of all the Russias.

Give a coward a gun, and, while he doesn't stop being a coward, it won't show in the same way. He may act like a violent, aggressive tyrant instead. That, of course, was why Ivan had been ecologically successful—in his specialized environment. He'd never run up against many stresses that brought his dominant trait to the fore. Like Disraeli, he had been able to control his environment so that such stresses were practically eliminated.

Martin turned green.

Then he remembered Erika. Could he get Erika to keep St. Cyr busy, somehow, while he got his contract release from Watt? As long as he could avoid crises, he could keep his nerve from crumbling, but—*there were assassins everywhere!*

Erika was on her way to the lot by now. Martin swallowed.

He would meet her outside the studio. The broom-closet wasn't safe. He could be trapped there like a rat—

"Nonsense," Martin told himself with shivering firmness. "This isn't me. All I have to do is get a g-grip on m-myself. Come, now. Buck up. *Toujours l'audace!"*

But he went out of his office and downstairs very softly and cautiously. After all, one never knew. And when every man's hand was against one. . . .

Quaking, the character-matrix of Ivan the Terrible stole toward a studio gate.

THE taxi drove rapidly toward Bel-Air.

"But what were you doing up that tree?" Erika demanded.

Martin shook violently.

"A werewolf," he chattered. "And a vampire and a ghoul and— I *saw* them, I tell you. There I was at the studio gate, and they all came at me in a mob."

"But they were just coming back from dinner," Erika said. "You know Summit's doing night shooting on *Abbott and Costello Meet Everybody*. Karloff wouldn't hurt a fly."

"I kept telling myself that," Martin said dully, "but I was out of my mind with guilt and fear. You see, I'm an abominable monster. But it's not my fault. It's environmental. I grew up in brutal and degrading conditions—oh, look!" He pointed toward a traffic cop ahead. "The police! Traitors even in the palace guards!"

"Lady, is that guy nuts?" the cabbie demanded.

"Mad or sane, I am Nicholas Martin," Martin announced, with an abrupt volte face. He tried to stand up commandingly, bumped his head, screamed *"Assassins!"* and burrowed into a corner of the seat, panting horribly.

Erika gave him a thoughtful, worried look.

"Nick," she said, "How much have you had to drink? What's wrong?"

Martin shut his eyes and lay back against the cushions.

"Let me have a few minutes, Erika," he pleaded. "I'll be all right as soon as I recover from stress. It's only when I'm under stress that Ivan—"

"You can accept your contract release from Watt, can't you? Surely you'll be able to manage that."

"Of course," Martin said with feeble bravery. He thought it over and reconsidered. "If I can hold your hand," he suggested, taking no chances.

This disgusted Erika so much that for two miles there was no more conversation within the cab.

Erika had been thinking her own thoughts.

"You've certainly changed since this morning," she observed. "Threatening to make love to me, of all things. As if I'd stand for it. I'd like to see you try." There was a pause. Erika slid her eyes sidewise toward Martin. "I said I'd like to see you try," she repeated.

"Oh, you would, would you?" Martin said with hollow valor. He paused. Oddly enough his tongue, hitherto frozen stiff on one particular subject in Erika's presence, was now thoroughly loosened. Martin wasted no time on theory. Seizing his chance before a new stress might unexpectedly arise, he instantly poured out his heart to Erika, who visibly softened.

"But why didn't you ever say so before?" she asked.

"I can't imagine," Martin said. "Then you'll marry me?"

"But why were you acting so—"

"Will you marry me?"

"Yes," Erika said, and there was a pause. Martin moistened his lips, discovering that somehow he and Erika had moved close together. He was about to seal the bargain in the customary manner when a sudden thought struck him and made him draw back with a little start.

Erika opened her eyes.

"Ah—" said Martin. "Um. I just happened to remember. There's a bad flu epidemic in Chicago. Epidemics spread like wildfire, you know. Why, it could be in Hollywood by now—especially with the prevailing westerly winds."

"I'm damned if I'm going to be proposed to and not kissed," Erika said in a somewhat irritated tone. "You kiss me!"

"But I might give you bubonic plague," Martin said nervously. "Kissing spreads germs. It's a well-known fact."

"Nick!"

"Well—I don't know—when did you last have a cold?"

Erika pulled away from him and went to sit in the other corner.

"Ah," Martin said, after a long silence. "Erika?"

"Don't talk to me, you miserable man," Erika said. "You monster, you."

"I can't help it," Martin cried wildly. "I'll be a coward for twelve hours. It's not my fault. After eight tomorrow morning I'll—I'll walk into a lion-cage if you want, but tonight I'm as yellow as Ivan the Terrible! At least let me tell you what's been happening."

Erika said nothing. Martin instantly plunged into his long and improbable tale.

"I don't believe a word of it," Erika said, when he had finished. She shook her head sharply. "Just the same, I'm still your agent, and your career's still my responsibility. The first and only thing we have to do is get your contract release from Tolliver Watt. And that's *all* we're going to consider right now, do you hear?"

"But St. Cyr—"

"I'll do all the talking. You won't have to say a word. If St. Cyr tries to bully you, I'll handle him. But you've got to be there with me, or St. Cyr will make that an excuse to postpone things again. I know him."

"Now I'm under stress again," Martin said wildly. "I can't stand it. *I'm* not the Tsar of Russia."

"Lady," said the cab-driver, looking back, "if I was you, I'd sure as hell break off that engagement."

"Heads will roll for this," Martin said ominously.

"BY mutual consent, agree to terminate . . . yes," Watt said, affixing his name to the legal paper that lay before him on the desk. "That does it. But where in the world is that fellow Martin?

He came in with you, I'm certain."

"Did he?" Erika asked, rather wildly. She too, was wondering how Martin had managed to vanish so miraculously from her side. Perhaps he had crept with lightning rapidity under the carpet. She forced her mind from the thought and reached for the contract release Watt was folding.

"Wait," St. Cyr said, his lower lip jutting. "What about a clause giving us an option on Martin's next play?"

Watt paused, and the director instantly struck home.

"Whatever it may be, I can turn it into a vehicle for DeeDee, eh, DeeDee?" He lifted a sausage finger at the lovely star, who nodded obediently.

"It's going to have an all-male cast," Erika said hastily. "And we're discussing contract releases, not options."

"He would give me an option if I had him here," St. Cyr growled, torturing his cigar horribly. "Why does everything conspire against an artist?" He waved a vast, hairy fist in the air. "Now I must break in a new writer, which is a great waste. Within a fortnight Martin would have been a St. Cyr writer. In fact, it is still possible."

"I'm afraid not, Raoul," Watt said resignedly. "You really shouldn't have hit Martin at the studio today."

"But—but he would not dare charge me with assault. In Mixo-Lydia—"

"Why, hello, Nick," DeeDee said, with a bright smile. "What are you hiding behind those curtains for?"

Every eye was turned toward the window draperies, just in time to see the white, terrified face of Nicholas Martin flip out of sight like a scared chipmunk's. Erika, her heart dropping, said hastily, "Oh, that isn't Nick. It doesn't look a bit like him. You made a mistake, DeeDee."

"Did I?" DeeDee asked, perfectly willing to agree.

"Certainly," Erika said, reaching for the contract release in Watt's hand. "Now if you'll just let me have this, I'll—"

"Stop!" cried St. Cyr in a bull's bellow. Head sunk between his heavy shoulders, he lumbered to the window and jerked the curtains aside.

"Ha!" the director said in a sinister voice. "Martin."

"It's a lie," Martin said feebly, making a desperate attempt to conceal his stress-triggered panic. "I've abdicated."

St. Cyr, who had stepped back a pace, was studying Martin carefully. Slowly the cigar in his mouth began to tilt upwards. An unpleasant grin widened the director's mouth.

He shook a finger under Martin's quivering nostrils.

"You!" he said. "Tonight it is a different tune, eh? Today you were drunk. Now I see it all. Valorous with pots, like they say."

"Nonsense," Martin said, rallying his courage by a glance at Erika. "Who say? Nobody but you would say a thing like that. Now what's this all about?"

"What were you doing behind that curtain?" Watt asked.

"*I* wasn't behind the curtain," Martin said, with great bravado. "*You* were. All of you. I was in front of the curtain. Can I help it if the whole lot of you conceal yourselves behind curtains in a library, like—like conspirators?" The word was unfortunately chosen. A panicky light flashed into Martin's eyes. "Yes, conspirators," he went on nervously. "You think I don't know, eh? Well, I do. You're all assassins, plotting and planning. So this is your headquarters, is it? All night your hired dogs have been at my heels, driving me like a wounded caribou to—"

"We've got to be going," Erika said desperately. "There's just time to catch the next carib—the next plane east." She reached for the contract release, but Watt suddenly put it in his pocket. He turned his chair toward Martin.

"Will you give us an option on your next play?" he demanded.

"Of course he will give us an option!" St. Cyr said, studying Martin's air of bravado with an experienced eye. "Also, there is to be no question of a charge of assault, for if there is I will beat you. So it is in Mixo-Lydia. In fact, you do not even want a release from your contract, Martin. It is all a mistake. I will turn you into a St. Cyr writer, and all will be well. So. Now you will ask Tolliver to tear up that release, will you not—*ha?*"

"Of course you won't, Nick," Erika cried. "Say so!"

THERE was a pregnant silence. Watt watched with sharp interest. So did the unhappy Erika, torn between her responsibility as Martin's agent and her disgust at the man's abject cowardice. DeeDee watched too, her eyes very wide and a cheerful smile upon her handsome face. But the battle was obviously between Martin and Raoul St. Cyr.

Martin drew himself up desperately. Now or never he must force himself to be truly Terrible. Already he had a troubled expression, just like Ivan. He strove to look sinister too. An enigmatic smile played around his lips. For an instant he resembled the Mad Tsar of Russia, except, of course, that he was clean-shaven. With contemptuous, regal power Martin stared down the Mixo-Lydian.

"You will tear up that release and sign an agreement giving us option on your next play too, ha?" St. Cyr said—but a trifle uncertainly.

"I'll do as I please," Martin told him. "How would you like to be eaten alive by dogs?"

"I don't know, Raoul," Watt said. "Let's try to get this settled even if—"

"Do you want me to go over to Metro and take DeeDee with me?" St. Cyr cried, turning toward Watt. "He *will* sign!" And, reaching into an inner pocket for a pen, the burly director swung back toward Martin.

"Assassin!" cried Martin, misinterpreting the gesture.

A gloating smile appeared on St. Cyr's revolting features.

"Now we have him, Tolliver," he said, with heavy triumph, and these ominous words added the final stress to Martin's overwhelming burden. With a mad cry he rushed past St. Cyr, wrenched open a door, and fled.

From behind him came Erika's Valkyrie voice.

"Leave him alone! Haven't you done enough already? Now I'm going to get that contract release from you before I leave this room, Tolliver Watt, and I warn you, St. Cyr, if you—"

But by then Martin was five rooms away, and the voice faded. He darted on, hopelessly trying to make himself slow down and return to the scene of battle. The pressure was too strong. Terror hurled him down a corridor, into another room, and against a metallic object from which he rebounded, to find himself sitting on the floor looking up at ENIAC Gamma the Ninety-Third.

"Ah, there you are," the robot said. "I've been searching all over spacetime for you. You forgot to give me a waiver of responsibility when you talked me into varying the experiment. The Authorities would be in my gears if I didn't bring back an eyeprinted waiver when a subject's scratched by variance."

With a frightened glance behind him, Martin rose to his feet.

"What?" he asked confusedly. "Listen, you've got to change me back to myself. Everyone's trying to kill me. You're just in time. I can't wait twelve hours. Change me back to myself, quick!"

"Oh, I'm through with you," the robot said callously. "You're no longer a suitably unconditioned subject, after that last treatment you insisted on. I should have got the waiver from you then, but you got me all confused with Disraeli's oratory. Now here. Just hold this up to your left eye for twenty seconds." He extended a flat, glittering little metal disk. "It's already sensitized and filled out. It only needs your eyeprint. Affix it, and you'll never see me again."

Martin shrank away.

"But what's going to happen to me?" he quavered, swallowing.

"How should I know? After twelve hours, the treatment will wear off, and you'll be yourself again. Hold this up to your eye, now."

"I will if you'll change me back to myself," Martin haggled.

"I can't. It's against the rules. One variance is bad enough, even with a filed waiver, but two? Oh, no. Hold this up to your left eye—"

"No," Martin said with feeble firmness. "I won't."

ENIAC studied him.

"Yes, you will," the robot said finally, "or I'll go boo at you."

Martin paled slightly, but he shook his head in desperate determination.

"No," he said doggedly. "Unless I get rid of Ivan's matrix right now, Erika will never marry me and I'll never get my contract release from Watt. All you have to do is put that helmet on my head and change me back to myself. Is that too much to ask?"

"Certainly, of a robot," ENIAC said stiffly. "No more shilly-shallying. It's lucky you are wearing the Ivan-matrix, so I can impose my will on you. Put your eyeprint on this. Instantly!"

Martin rushed behind the couch and hid. The robot advanced menacingly. And at that moment, pushed to the last ditch, Martin suddenly remembered something.

He faced the robot.

"WAIT," he said. "You don't understand. I can't eyeprint that thing. It won't work on me. Don't you realize that? It's supposed to take the eyeprint—"

"—of the rod-and-cone pattern of the retina," the robot said. "So—"

"So how can it do that unless I can keep my eye open for twenty seconds? My perceptive reaction-thresholds are Ivan's aren't they? I can't control the reflex of blinking. I've got a coward's synapses. And they'd force me to shut my eyes tight the second that gimmick got too close to them."

"Hold them open," the robot suggested. "With your fingers."

"My fingers have reflexes too," Martin argued, moving toward a sideboard. "There's only one answer. I've got to get drunk. If I'm half stupefied with liquor, my reflexes will be so slow I won't be able to shut my eyes. And don't try to use force, either. If I dropped dead with fear, how could you get my eyeprint then?"

"Very easily," the robot said. "I'd pry open your lids—"

Martin hastily reached for a bottle on the sideboard, and a glass. But his hand swerved aside and gripped, instead, a siphon of soda water.

"—only," ENIAC went on, "the forgery might be detected."

Martin fizzled the glass full of soda and took a long drink.

"I won't be long getting drunk," he said, his voice thickening. "In fact, it's beginning to work already. See? I'm coöperating."

The robot hesitated.

"Well, hurry up about it," he said, and sat down.

Martin, about to take another drink, suddenly paused, staring at ENIAC. Then, with a sharply indrawn breath, he lowered the glass.

"What's the matter now?" the robot asked. "Drink your —what is it?"

"It's whiskey," Martin told the inexperienced automaton, "but now I see it all. You've put poison in it. So that's your plan, is it? Well, I won't touch another drop, and now you'll never get my eyeprint. I'm no fool."

"Cog Almighty," the robot said, rising. "You poured that drink yourself. How could I have poisoned it? Drink!"

"I won't," Martin said, with a coward's stubbornness, fighting back the growing suspicion that the drink might really be toxic.

"You swallow that drink,"

ENIAC commanded, his voice beginning to quiver slightly. "It's perfectly harmless."

"Then prove it!" Martin said cunningly. "Would you be willing to switch glasses? Would you drink this poisoned brew yourself?"

"How do you expect me to drink?" the robot demanded. "I—" He paused. "All right, hand me the glass," he said. "I'll take a sip. Then you've got to drink the rest of it."

"Aha!" Martin said. "You betrayed yourself that time. You're a robot. You can't drink, remember? Not the same way that I can, anyhow. Now I've got you trapped, you assassin. *There's* your brew." He pointed to a floor-lamp. "Do you dare to drink with me now, in your electrical fashion, or do you admit you are trying to poison me? Wait a minute, what am I saying? That wouldn't prove a—"

"Of course it would," the robot said hastily. "You're perfectly right, and it's very cunning of you. We'll drink together, and that will prove your whiskey's harmless—so you'll keep on drinking till your reflexes slow down, see?"

"Well," Martin began uncertainly, but the unscrupulous robot unscrewed a bulb from the floor lamp, pulled the switch, and inserted his finger into the empty socket, which caused a crackling flash. "There," the robot said. "It isn't poisoned, see?"

"You're not swallowing it," Martin said suspiciously. "You're holding it in your mouth—I mean your finger."

ENIAC again probed the socket.

"Well, all right, perhaps," Martin said, in a doubtful fashion. "But I'm not going to risk your slipping a powder in my liquor, you traitor. You're going to keep up with me, drink for drink, until I can eyeprint that gimmick of yours—or else I stop drinking. But does sticking your finger in that lamp really prove my liquor isn't poisoned? I can't quite—"

"Of course it does," the robot said quickly. "I'll prove it. I'll do it again . . . *f(t)*. Powerful DC, isn't it? Certainly it proves it. Keep drinking, now."

HIS gaze watchfully on the robot, Martin lifted his glass of club soda.

"Fffff(t)!" cried the robot, some time later, sketching a singularly loose smile on its metallic face.

"Best fermented mammoth's milk I ever tasted," Martin agreed, lifting his tenth glass of soda-water. He felt slightly queasy and wondered if he might be drowning.

"Mammoth's milk?" asked ENIAC thickly. "What year is this?"

Martin drew a long breath. Ivan's capacious memory had served him very well so far. Voltage, he recalled, increased the frequency of the robot's thought-patterns and disorganized ENIAC's memory—which was being proved before his eyes. But the crux of his plan was yet to come. . . .

"The year of the great Hairy One, of course," Martin said briskly. "Don't you remember?"

"Then you—" ENIAC strove to focus upon his drinking-companion. "You must be Mammoth-Slayer."

"That's it!" Martin cried. "Have another jolt. What about giving me the treatment now?"

"What treatment?"

Martin looked impatient. "You said you were going to impose the character-matrix of Mammoth-Slayer on my mind. You said *that* would insure my optimum ecological adjustment in this temporal phase, and nothing else would."

"Did I? But you're not Mammoth-Slayer," ENIAC said confusedly. "Mammoth-Slayer was the son of the Great Hairy One. What's your mother's name?"

"The Great Hairy One," Martin replied, at which the robot grated its hand across its gleaming forehead.

"Have one more jolt," Martin suggested. "Now take out the ecologizer and put it on my head."

"Like this?" ENIAC asked, obeying. "I keep feeling I've forgotten something important. *F (t).*"

Martin adjusted the crystal helmet on his skull. "Now," he commanded. "Give me the character-matrix of Mammoth-Slayer, son of the Great Hairy One."

"Well—all right," ENIAC said dizzily. The red ribbons swirled. There was a flash from the helmet. "There," the robot said. "It's done. It may take a few minutes to begin functioning, but then for twelve hours you'll—wait! Where are you going?"

But Martin had already departed.

The robot stuffed the helmet and the quarter-mile of red ribbon back for the last time. He lurched to the floor-lamp, muttering something about one for the road. Afterward, the room lay empty. A fading murmur said, *"F(t)."*

"NICK!" Erika gasped, staring at the figure in the doorway. "Don't stand like that! You frighten me!"

Everyone in the room looked up abruptly at her cry, and so were just in time to see a horrifying change take place in Martin's shape. It was an illusion, of course, but an alarming one. His knees slowly bent until he was half-crouching, his shoulders slumped as though bowed by the weight of enormous back and shoulder muscles, and his arms swung forward until their knuckles hung perilously near the floor.

Nicholas Martin had at last achieved a personality whose ecological norm would put him on a level with Raoul St. Cyr.

"Nick!" Erika quavered.

Slowly Martin's jaw protruded till his lower teeth were hideously visible. Gradually his eyelids dropped until he was peering up out of tiny, wicked sockets. Then, slowly, a perfectly shocking grin broadened Mr. Martin's mouth.

"Erika," he said throatily. "Mine!"

And with that, he shambled forward, seized the horrified girl in his arms, and bit her on the ear.

"Oh, Nick," Erika murmured, closing her eyes. "Why didn't you ever—no, no, *no!* Nick! Stop it! The contract release. We've got to—Nick, what are you doing?" She snatched at Martin's departing form, but too late.

For all his ungainly and unpleasant gait, Martin covered ground fast. Almost instantly he was clambering over Watt's desk as the most direct route to that startled tycoon. DeeDee looked on, a little surprised. St. Cyr lunged forward.

"In Mixo-Lydia—" he began. "Ha! So!" He picked up Martin and threw him across the room.

"Oh, you beast," Erika cried, and flung herself upon the director, beating at his brawny chest. On second thought, she used her shoes on his shins with more effect. St. Cyr, no gentleman, turned her around, pinioned her arms behind her, and glanced up at Watt's alarmed cry.

"Martin! What are you doing?"

There was reason for his inquiry. Apparently unhurt by St. Cyr's toss, Martin had hit the floor, rolled over and over like a ball, knocked down a floor-lamp with a crash, and uncurled, with an unpleasant expression on his face. He rose crouching, bandy-legged, his arms swinging low, a snarl curling his lips.

"You take my mate?" the pithecanthropic Mr. Martin inquired throatily, rapidly losing all touch with the twentieth century. It was a rhetorical question. He picked up the lamp-standard—he did not have to bend to do it—tore off the silk shade as he would have peeled foliage from a tree-limb, and balanced the weapon in his hand. Then he moved forward, carrying the lamp-standard like a spear.

"I," said Martin, "kill."

He then endeavored, with the most admirable singleheartedness, to carry out his expressed intention. The first thrust of the blunt, improvised spear rammed into St. Cyr's solar plexus and drove him back against the wall with a booming thud. This seemed to be what Martin wanted. Keeping one end of his spear pressed into the director's belly, he crouched lower, dug his toes into the rug, and did his very best to drill a hole in St. Cyr.

"Stop it!" cried Watt, flinging himself into the conflict. Ancient reflexes took over. Martin's arm shot out. Watt shot off in the opposite direction.

The lamp broke.

Martin looked pensively at the pieces, tentatively began to bite one, changed his mind, and looked at St. Cyr instead. The gasping director, mouthing threats, curses and objections, drew himself up, and shook a huge fist at Martin.

"I," he announced, "shall kill you with my bare hands. Then I go over to MGM with DeeDee. In Mixo-Lydia—"

Martin lifted his own fists toward his face. He regarded them. He unclenched them slowly, while a terrible grin spread across his face. And then, with every tooth showing, and with the hungry gleam of a mad tiger in his tiny little eyes, he lifted his gaze to St. Cyr's throat.

Mammoth-Slayer was not the son of the Great Hairy One for nothing.

MARTIN sprang.

So did St. Cyr—in another direction, screaming with sudden terror. For, after all, he was only a medievalist. The feudal man is far more civilized than the so-called man of Mammoth-Slayer's primordially direct era, and as a man recoils from a small but murderous wildcat, so St. Cyr fled in sudden civilized horror from an attacker who was, literally, afraid of nothing.

He sprang through the window and, shrieking, vanished into the night.

Martin was taken by surprise. When Mammoth-Slayer leaped at an enemy, the enemy leaped at him too, and so Martin's head slammed against the wall with disconcerting force. Dimly he heard diminishing, terrified cries. Laboriously he crawled to his feet and set back against the wall, snarling, quite ready. . . .

"Nick!" Erika's voice called. "Nick, it's me! Stop it! *Stop it!* DeeDee—"

"Ugh?" Martin said thickly, shaking his head. "Kill." He growled softly, blinking through red-rimmed little eyes at the scene around him. It swam back slowly into focus. Erika was struggling with DeeDee near the window.

"You let me go," DeeDee cried. "Where Raoul goes, I go."

"DeeDee!" pleaded a new voice. Martin glanced aside to see Tolliver Watt crumpled in a corner, a crushed lampshade half obscuring his face.

With a violent effort Martin straightened up. Walking upright seemed unnatural, somehow, but it helped submerge Mammoth-Slayer's worst instincts. Besides, with St. Cyr gone, stresses were slowly subsiding, so that Mammoth-Slayer's dominant trait was receding from the active foreground.

Martin tested his tongue cautiously, relieved to find he was still capable of human speech.

"Uh," he said. "Arrgh . . . ah. Watt."

Watt blinked at him anxiously through the lampshade.

"Urgh . . . Ur—release," Martin said, with a violent effort. "Contract release. Gimme."

Watt had courage. He crawled to his feet, removing the lamp-shade.

"Contract release!" he snapped. "You madman! Don't you realize what you've done? DeeDee's walking out on me. DeeDee, don't go. We will bring Raoul back—"

"Raoul told me to quit if he quit," Dee Dee said stubbornly.

"You don't have to do what St. Cyr tells you," Erika said, hanging onto the struggling star.

"Don't I?" DeeDee asked, astonished. "Yes, I do. I always have."

"DeeDee," Watt said frantically, "I'll give you the finest contract on earth—a ten-year contract—look, here it is." He tore out a well-creased document. "All you have to do is sign, and you can have anything you want Wouldn't you like that?"

"Oh, yes," DeeDee said. "But Raoul wouldn't like it." She broke free from Erika.

"Martin!" Watt told the playwright frantically, "Get St. Cyr back. Apologize to him. I don't care how, but get him back! If you don't, I—I'll never give you your release."

Martin was observed to slump slightly—perhaps with hopelessness. Then, again, perhaps not.

"I'm sorry," DeeDee said. "I liked working for you, Tolliver. But I have to do what Raoul says, of course." And she moved toward the window.

Martin had slumped further down, till his knuckles quite brushed the rug. His angry little eyes, glowing with baffled rage, were fixed on DeeDee. Slowly his lips peeled back, exposing every tooth in his head.

"You," he said, in an ominous growl.

DeeDee paused, but only briefly.

THEN the enraged roar of a wild beast reverberated through the room. *"You come back!"* bellowed the infuriated Mammoth-Slayer, and with one agile bound sprang to the window, seized DeeDee and slung her under one arm. Wheeling, he glared jealously at the shrinking Watt and reached for Erika. In a trice he had the struggling forms of both girls captive, one under each arm. His wicked little eyes glanced from one to another. Then, playing no favorites, he bit each quickly on the ear.

"Nick!" Erika cried. "How dare you!"

"Mine," Mammoth-Slayer informed her hoarsely.

"You bet I am," Erika said, "but that works both ways. Put down that hussy you've got under your other arm."

Mammoth-Slayer was observed to eye DeeDee doubtfully.

"Well," Erika said tartly, "make up your mind."

"Both," said the uncivilized playwright. "Yes."

"No!" Erika said.

"Yes," DeeDee breathed in an entirely new tone. Limp as a dishrag, the lovely creature hung from Martin's arm and gazed up at her captor with idolatrous admiration.

"Oh, you hussy," Erika said. "What about St. Cyr?"

"Him," DeeDee said scornfully. "He hasn't got a thing, the sissy. I'll never look at him again." She turned her adoring gaze back to Martin.

"Pah," the latter grunted, tossing DeeDee into Watt's lap. "Yours. Keep her." He grinned approvingly at Erika. "Strong she. Better."

Both Watt and DeeDee remained motionless, staring at Martin.

"You," he said, thrusting a finger at DeeDee. "You stay with him. Ha?" He indicated Watt.

DeeDee nodded in slavish adoration.

"You sign contract?"

Nod.

Martin looked significantly into Watt's eyes. He extended his hand.

"The contract release," Erika explained, upside-down. "Give it to him before he pulls your head off."

Slowly Watt pulled the contract release from his pocket and held it out. But Martin was already shambling toward the window. Erika reached back hastily and snatched the document.

"That was a wonderful act," she told Nick, as they reached the street. "Put me down now. We can find a cab some—"

"No act," Martin growled. "Real. Till tomorrow. After that—" He shrugged. "But tonight, Mammoth-Slayer."

He attempted to climb a palm tree, changed his mind, and shambled on, carrying the now pensive Erika. But it was not until a police car drove past that Erika screamed. . . .

"I'LL bail you out tomorrow," Erika told Mammoth-Slayer, struggling between two large patrolmen.

Her words were drowned in an infuriated bellow.

Thereafter events blurred, to solidify again for the irate Mammoth-Slayer only when he was thrown in a cell, where he picked himself up with a threatening roar. "I kill!" he announced, seizing the bars. "*Arrrgh!*"

"Two in one night," said a bored voice, moving away outside. "Both in Bel-Air, too. Think they're hopped up? We couldn't get a coherent story out of either one."

The bars shook. An annoyed voice from one of the bunks said to shut up, and added that there had been already enough trouble from nincompoops without—here it paused, hesitated, and uttered a shrill, sharp, piercing cry.

Silence prevailed, momentarily, in the cell-block as Mammoth-Slayer, son of the Great Hairy One, turned slowly to face Raoul St. Cyr.

TO EACH HIS STAR

by BRYCE WALTON

"Nothing around those other suns but ashes and dried blood," old Dunbar told the space-wrecked, desperate men. "Only one way to go, where we can float down through the clouds to Paradise. That's straight ahead to the sun with the red rim around it."

But Dunbar's eyes were old and uncertain. How could they believe in his choice when every star in this forsaken section of space was surrounded by a beckoning red rim?

THERE was just blackness, frosty glimmering terrible blackness, going out and out forever in all directions. Russell didn't think they could remain sane in all this blackness much longer. Bitterly he thought of how they would die—not knowing within maybe thousands of light years where they were, or where they were going.

After the wreck, the four of them had floated a while, floated and drifted together, four men in bulbous pressure suits like small individual

rockets, held together by an awful pressing need for each other and by the "gravity-rope" beam.

Dunbar, the oldest of the four, an old space-buster with a face wrinkled like a dried prune, burned by cosmic rays and the suns of worlds so far away they were scarcely credible, had taken command. Suddenly, Old Dunbar had known where they were. Suddenly, Dunbar knew where they were going.

They could talk to one another through the etheric transmitters inside their helmets. They could live . . . if this was living . . . a long time, if only a man's brain would hold up, Russell thought. The suits were complete units. 700 pounds each, all enclosing shelters, with atmosphere pressure, temperature control, mobility in space, and electric power. Each suit had its own power-plant, reprocessing continuously the precious air breathed by the occupants, putting it back into circulation again after enriching it. Packed with food concentrates. Each suit a rocket, each human being part of a rocket, and the special "life-gun" that went with each suit each blast of which sent a man a few hundred thousand miles further on toward wherever he was going.

Four men, thought Russell, held together by an invisible string of gravity, plunging through a lost pocket of hell's dark where there had never been any sound or life, with old Dunbar the first in line, taking the lead because he was older and knew where he was and where he was going. Maybe Johnson, second in line, and Alvar who was third, knew too, but were afraid to admit it.

But Russell knew it and he'd admitted it from the first —that old Dunbar was as crazy as a Jovian juke-bird.

A lot of time had rushed past into darkness. Russell had no idea now how long the four of them had been plunging toward the red-rimmed sun that never seemed to get any nearer. When the ultra-drive had gone crazy the four of them had blanked out and nobody could say now how long an interim that had been. Nobody knew what happened to a man who suffered a space-time warping like that. When they had regained consciousness, the ship was pretty banged up, and the meteor-repellor shields cracked. A meteor ripped the ship down the center like an old breakfast cannister.

How long ago that had been, Russell didn't know. All Russell knew was that they were millions of light years from any place he had ever heard about, where the galactic space lanterns had absolutely no recognizable pattern. But Dunbar knew. And Russell was looking at Dunbar's suit up ahead, watching it more and more intently, thinking about how Dunbar looked inside that suit—and hating Dunbar more and more for claiming he knew when he didn't, for his drooling optimism—because he was taking them on into deeper darkness and calling their destination Paradise.

Russell wanted to laugh, but the last time he'd given way to this impulse, the results inside his helmet had been too unpleasant to repeat.

Sometimes Russell thought of other things besides his growing hatred of the old man. Sometimes he thought about the ship, lost back there in the void, and he wondered if wrecked space ships were ever found. Compared with the universe in which one of them drifted, a wrecked ship was a lot smaller than a grain of sand on a nice warm beach back on Earth, or one of those specks of silver dust that floated like strange seeds down the night winds of Venus.

And a human was smaller still, thought Russell when he was not hating Dunbar. Out here, a human being is the smallest thing of all. He thought then of what Dunbar would say to such a thought, how Dunbar would laugh that high piping squawking laugh of his and say that the human being was bigger than the Universe itself.

Dunbar had a big answer for every little thing.

When the four of them had escaped from that prison colony on a sizzling hot asteroid rock in the Ronlwhyn system, that wasn't enough for Dunbar. Hell no—Dunbar had to start talking about a place they could go where they'd never be apprehended, in a system no one else had ever heard of, where they could live like gods on a green soft world like the Earth had been a long time back.

And Dunbar had spouted endlessly about a world of treasure they would find, if they would just follow old Dunbar. That's what all four of them had been trying to find all their lives in the big cold grabbag of eternity—a rich star, a rich far fertile star where no one else had ever been, loaded with treasure that had no name, that no one had ever heard of before. And was, because of that, the richest treasure of all.

We all look alike out here in these big rocket pressure suits, Russell thought. No one for God only knew how many of millions of light years away could see or care. Still—we might have a chance to live, even now, Russell thought—if it weren't for old crazy Dunbar.

They might have a chance if Alvar and Johnson weren't so damn lacking in self-confidence as to put all their trust in that crazed old rum-dum. Russell had known now for some time that they were going in the wrong direction. No reason for knowing. Just a hunch. And Russell was sure his hunch was right.

RUSSELL said. "Look—look to your left and to your right and behind us. Four suns. You guys see those other three suns all around you, don't you?"

"Sure," someone said.

"Well, if you'll notice," Russell said, "the one on the left also now has a red rim around it. Can't you guys see that?"

"Yeah, I see it," Alvar said.

"So now," Johnson said, "there's two suns with red rims around them."

"We're about in the middle of those four suns aren't we, Dunbar?" Russell said.

"That's right, boys!" yelled old Dunbar in that sickeningly optimistic voice. Like a hysterical old woman's. "Just about in the sweet dark old middle."

"You're still sure it's the sun up ahead . . . that's the only one with life on it, Dunbar . . . the only one we can live on?" Russell asked.

"That's right! That's right," Dunbar yelled. "That's the only one—and it's a paradise. Not just a place to live, boys—but a place you'll have trouble believing in because it's like a dream!"

"And none of these other three suns have worlds we could live on, Dunbar?" Russell asked. Keep the old duck talking like this and maybe Alvar and Johnson would see that he was cracked.

"Yeah," said Alvar. "You still say that, Dunbar?"

"No life, boys, nothing," Dunbar laughed. "Nothing on these other worlds but ashes . . . just ashes and iron and dried blood, dried a million years or more."

"When in hell were you ever here?" Johnson said. "You say you were here before. You never said when, or why or anything!"

"It was a long time back boys. Don't remember too well, but it was when we had an old ship called the DOG STAR that I was here. A pirate ship and I was second in command, and we came through this sector. That was —hell, it musta' been fifty years ago. I been too many places nobody's ever bothered to name or chart, to remember where it is, but I been here. I remember those four suns all spotted to form a perfect circle from this point, with us squarely in the middle. We explored all these suns and the worlds that go round 'em. Trust me, boys, and we'll reach the right one. And that one's just like Paradise."

"Paradise is it," Russell whispered hoarsely.

"Paradise and there we'll be like gods, like Mercuries with wings flying on nights of sweet song. These other suns, don't let them bother you. They're jezebels of stars. All painted up in the darkness and pretty and waiting and calling and lying! They make you think of nice green worlds all running waters and dews and forests thick as fleas on a wet dog. But it ain't there, boys. I know this place. I been here, long time back."

Russell said tightly. "It'll take us a long time won't it? If it's got air we can breath, and water we can drink and shade we can rest in—that'll be paradise enough for us. But it'll take a long time won't it? And what if it isn't there—what if after all the time we spend hoping and getting there—there won't be nothing but ashes and cracked clay?"

"I know we're going right," Dunbar said cheerfully. "I can tell. Like I said—you can tell it because of the red rim around it."

"But the sun on our left, you can see—it's got a red rim too now," Russell said.

"Yeah, that's right," said Alvar. "Sometimes I see a red rim around the one we're going for, sometimes a red rim around that one on the left. Now, sometimes I'm not sure either of them's got a red rim. You said that one had a red rim, Dunbar, and I wanted to believe it. So now maybe we're all seeing a red rim that was never there."

Old Dunbar laughed. The sound brought blood hotly to Russell's face. "We're heading to the right one, boys. Don't doubt me . . . I been here. We explored all these sun systems. And I remember it all. The second planet from that red-rimmed sun. You come down through a soft atmosphere, floating like in a dream. You see the green lakes coming up through the clouds and the women dancing and the music playing. I remember seeing a ship there that brought those women there, a long long time before ever I got there. A land like heaven and women like angels singing and dancing and laughing with red lips and arms white as milk, and soft silky hair floating in the winds."

Russell was very sick of the old man's voice. He was at least glad he didn't have to look at the old man now. His bald head, his skinny bobbing neck, his simpering watery blue eyes. But he still had to suffer that immutable babbling, that idiotic cheerfulness . . . and knowing all the time the old man was crazy, that he was leading them wrong.

I'd break away, go it alone to the right sun, Russell thought—but I'd never make it alone. A little while out here alone and I'd be nuttier than old Dunbar will ever be, even if he keeps on getting nuttier all the time.

Somewhere, sometime then . . . Russell got the idea that the only way was to get rid of Dunbar.

"YOU mean to tell us there are people living by that red-rimmed sun," Russell said.

"Lost people . . . lost . . . who knows how long," Dunbar said, as the four of them hurtled along. "You never know where you'll find people on a world somewhere nobody's ever named or knows about. Places where a lost ship's landed and never got up again, or wrecked itself so far off the lanes they'll never be found except by accident for millions of years. That's what this world is, boys. Must have been a ship load of beautiful people, maybe actresses and people like that being hauled to some outpost to entertain. They're like angels now, living in a land all free from care. Every place you see green forests and fields and blue lakes, and at nights there's three moons that come around the sky in a thousand different colors. And it never gets cold . . . it's always spring, always spring, boys, and the music plays all night, every night of a long long year. . . ."

Russell suddenly shouted. "Keep quiet, Dunbar. Shut up will you?"

Johnson said. "Dunbar—how long'll it take us?"

"Six months to a year, I'd say," Dunbar yelled happily. "That is—of our hereditary time."

"What?" croaked Alvar.

Johnson didn't say anything at all.

Russell screamed at Dunbar, then quieted down. He whispered. "Six months to a year—out here—cooped up in these damn suits. You're crazy as hell, Dunbar. Crazy . . . crazy! Nobody could stand it. We'll all be crazier than you are—"

"We'll make it, boys. Trust ole' Dunbar. What's a year when we know we're getting to Paradise at the end of it? What's a year out here . . . it's paradise ain't it, compared with that prison hole we were rotting in? We can make it. We have the food concentrates, and all the rest. All we need's the will, boys, and we got that. The whole damn Universe isn't big enough to kill the will of a human being, boys. I been over a whole lot of it, and I know. In the old days—"

"The hell with the old days," screamed Russell.

"Now quiet down, Russ," Dunbar said in a kind of dreadful crooning whisper. "You calm down now. You younger fellows—you don't look at things the way we used to. Thing is, we got to go straight. People trapped like this liable to start meandering. Liable to start losing the old will-power."

He chuckled.

"Yeah," said Alvar. "Someone says maybe we ought to go left, and someone says to go right, and someone else says to go in another direction. And then someone says maybe they'd better go back the old way. An' pretty soon something breaks, or the food runs out, and you're a million million miles from someplace you don't care about any more because you're dead. All frozen up in space . . . preserved like a piece of meat in a cold storage locker. And then maybe in a million years or so some lousy insect man from Jupiter comes along and finds you and takes you away to a museum. . . ."

"Shut up!" Johnson yelled.

Dunbar laughed. "Boys, boys, don't get panicky. Keep your heads. Just stick to old Dunbar and he'll see you through. I'm always lucky. Only one way to go . . . an' that's straight ahead to the sun with the red-rim around it . . . and then we tune in the gravity repellors, and coast down, floating and singing down through the clouds to paradise."

After that they traveled on for what seemed months to Russell, but it couldn't have been over a day or two of the kind of time-sense he had inherited from Earth.

Then he saw how the other two stars also were beginning to develop red rims. He yelled this fact out to the others. And Alvar said. "Russ's right. That sun to the right, and the one behind us . . . now they ALL have red rims around them. Dunbar—" A pause and no awareness of motion.

Dunbar laughed. "Sure, they all maybe have a touch of red, but it isn't the same, boys. I can tell the difference. Trust me—"

Russell half choked on his words. "You old goat! With those old eyes of yours, you couldn't see your way into a fire!"

"Don't get panicky now. Keep your heads. In another year, we'll be there—"

"God, you gotta' be sure," Alvar said. "I don't mind dyin' out here. But after a year of this, and then to get to a world that was only ashes, and not able to go any further—"

"I always come through, boys. I'm lucky. Angel women will take us to their houses on the edges of cool lakes, little houses that sit there in the sun like fancy jewels. And we'll walk under colored fountains, pretty colored fountains just splashing and splashing like pretty rain on our hungry hides. That's worth waiting for."

Russell did it before he hardly realized he was killing the old man. It was something he had had to do for a long time and that made it easy. There was a flash of burning oxygen from inside the suit of Dunbar. If he'd aimed right, Russell knew the fire-bullet should have pierced Dunbar's back. Now the fire was gone, extinguished automatically by units inside the suit. The suit was still inflated, self-sealing. Nothing appeared to have changed. The four of them hurtling on together, but inside that first suit up there on the front of the gravity rope, Dunbar was dead.

He was dead and his mouth was shut for good.

Dunbar's last faint cry from inside his suit still rang in Russell's ears, and he knew Alvar and Johnson had heard it too. Alvar and Johnson both called Dunbar's name a few times. There was no answer.

"Russ—you shouldn't have done that," Johnson whispered. "You shouldn't have done that to the old man!"

"No," Alvar said, so low he could barely be heard. "You shouldn't have done it."

"I did it for the three of us," Russell said. "It was either him or us. Lies . . . lies that was all he had left in his crazy head. Paradise . . . don't tell me you guys don't see the red rims around all four suns, all four suns all around us. Don't tell me you guys didn't know he was batty, that you really believed all that stuff he was spouting all the time!"

"Maybe he was lying, maybe not," Johnson said. "Now he's dead anyway."

"Maybe he was wrong, crazy, full of lies," Alvar said. "But now he's dead."

"How could he see any difference in those four stars?" Russell said, louder.

"He thought he was right," Alvar said. "He wanted to take us to paradise. He was happy, nothing could stop the old man—but he's dead now."

He sighed.

"He was taking us wrong . . . wrong!" Russell screamed. "Angels—music all night—houses like jewels—and women like angels—"

"Shhhh," said Alvar. It was quiet. How could it be so quiet, Russell thought? And up ahead the old man's pressure suit with a corpse inside went on ahead, leading the other three at the front of the gravity-rope.

"Maybe he was wrong," Alvar said. "But now do we know which way is right?"

SOMETIME later, Johnson said, "We got to decide now. Let's forget the old man. Let's forget him and all that's gone and let's start now and decide what to do."

And Alvar said, "Guess he was crazy all right, and I guess we trusted him because we didn't have the strength to make up our own minds. Why does a crazy man's laugh sound so good when you're desperate and don't know what to do?"

"I always had a feeling we were going wrong," Johnson said. "Anyway, it's forgotten, Russ. It's swallowed up in the darkness all around. It's never been."

Russell said, "I've had a hunch all along that maybe the old man was here before, and that he was right about there being a star here with a world we can live on. But I've known we was heading wrong. I've had a hunch all along that the right star was the one to the left."

"I don't know," Johnson sighed. "I been feeling partial toward that one on the right. What about you, Alvar?"

"I always thought we were going straight in the opposite direction from what we should, I guess. I always wanted to turn around and go back. It won't make over maybe a month's difference. And what does a month matter anyway out here—hell there never was any time out here until we came along. We make our own time here, and a month don't matter to me."

Sweat ran down Russell's face. His voice trembled. "No—that's wrong. You're both wrong." He could see himself going it alone. Going crazy because he was alone. He'd have broken away, gone his own direction, long ago but for that fear.

"How can we tell which of us is right?" Alvar said. "It's like everything was changing all the time out here. Sometimes I'd swear none of those suns had red rims, and at other times—like the old man said, they're all pretty and lying and saying nothing, just changing all the time. Jezebel stars, the old man said."

"I know I'm right," Russell pleaded. "My hunches always been right. My hunch got us out of that prison didn't it? Listen—I tell you it's that star to the left—"

"The one to the right," said Johnson.

"We been going away from the right one all the time," said Alvar.

"We got to stay together," said Russell. "Nobody could spend a year out here . . . alone. . . ."

"Ah . . . in another month or so we'd be lousy company anyway," Alvar said. "Maybe a guy could get to the point where he'd sleep most of the time . . . just wake up enough times to give himself another boost with the old life-gun."

"We got to face it," Johnson said finally. "We three don't go on together any more."

"That's it," said Alvar. "There's three suns that look like they might be right seeing as how we all agree the old man was wrong. But we believe there is one we can live by, because we all seem to agree that the old man might have been right about that. If we stick together, the chance is three to one against us. But if each of us makes for one star, one of us has a chance to live. Maybe not in paradise like the old man said, but a place where we can live.. And maybe there'll be intelligent life, maybe even a ship, and whoever gets the right star can come and help the other two. . . ."

"No . . . God no. . . ." Russell whispered over and over. "None of us can ever make it alone. . . ."

Alvar said, "We each take the star he likes best. I'll go back the other way. Russ, you take the left. And you, Johnson, go to the right."

Johnson started to laugh. Russell was yelling wildly at them, and above his own yelling he could hear Johnson's rising laughter. "Every guy's got a star of his own," Johnson said when he stopped laughing. "And we got ours. A nice red-rimmed sun for each of us to call his very own."

"Okay," Alvar said. "We cut off the gravity rope, and each to his own sun."

Now Russell wasn't saying anything.

"And the old man," Alvar said, "can keep right on going toward what he thought was right. And he'll keep on going. Course he won't be able to give himself another boost with the life-gun, but he'll keep going. Someday he'll get to that red-rimmed star of his. Out here in space, once you're going, you never stop . . . and I guess there isn't any other body to pull him off his course. And what will time matter to old Dunbar? Even less than to us, I guess. He's dead and he won't care."

"Ready," Johnson said. "I'll cut off the gravity rope."

"I'm ready," Alvar said. "To go back toward whatever it was I started from."

"Ready, Russ?"

Russell couldn't say anything. He stared at the endless void which now he would share with no one. Not even crazy old Dunbar.

"All right," Johnson said. "Good-bye."

Russell felt the release, felt the sudden inexplicable isolation and aloneness even before Alvar and Johnson used their life-guns and shot out of sight, Johnson toward the left and Alvar back toward that other red-rimmed sun behind them.

And old Dunbar shooting right on ahead. And all three of them dwindling and dwindling and blinking out like little lights.

Fading, he could hear their voices. "Each to his own star," Johnson said. "On a bee line."

"On a bee line," Alvar said.

Russell used his own life-gun and in a little while he didn't hear Alvar or Johnson's voices, nor could he see them. They were thousands of miles away, and going further all the time.

Russell's head fell forward against the front of his helmet, and he closed his eyes. "Maybe," he thought, "I shouldn't have killed the old man. Maybe one sun's as good as another. . . ."

Then he raised his body and looked out into the year of blackness that waited for him, stretching away to the red-rimmed sun. Even if he were right—he was sure now he'd never make it alone.

THE body inside the pressure suit drifted into a low-level orbit around the second planet from the sun of its choice, and drifted there a long time. A strato-cruiser detected it by chance because of the strong concentration of radio-activity that came from it.

They took the body down to one of the small, quiet towns on the edge of one of the many blue lakes where the domed houses were like bright joyful jewels. They got the leathery, well-preserved body from the pressure suit.

"An old man," one of them mused. "A very old man. From one of the lost sectors.

I wonder how and why he came so very far from his home?"

"Wrecked a ship out there, probably," one of the others said. "But he managed to get this far. It looks as though a small meteor fragment pierced his body. Here. You see?"

"Yes," another of them said. "But what amazes me is that this old man picked this planet out of all the others. The only one in this entire sector that would sustain life."

"Maybe he was just a very lucky old man. Yes . . . a man who attains such an age was usually lucky. Or at least that is what they say about the lost sectors."

"Maybe he knew the way here. Maybe he was here before—sometime."

The other shook his head. "I don't think so. They say some humans from that far sector did land here—but that's probably only a myth. And if they did, it was well over a thousand years ago."

Another said. "He has a fine face, this old man. A noble face. Whoever he is . . . wherever he came from, he died bravely and he knew the way, though he never reached this haven of the lost alive."

"Nor is it irony that he reached here dead," said the Lake Chieftain. He had been listening and he stepped forward and raised his arm. "He was old. It is obvious that he fought bravely, that he had great courage, and that he knew the way. He will be given a burial suitable to his stature, and he will rest here among the brave.

"Let the women dance and the music play for this old man. Let the trumpets speak, and the rockets fly up. And let flowers be strewn over the path above which the women will carry him to rest."

Calling All Fans

THE BIGGEST EVENT in science fiction is the annual World Science Fiction Convention. There fans, authors, artists, editors, and casual readers can all get together on an equal footing. Auctions, speeches, a banquet and other business are transacted. But the primary purpose is that everyone should have a good time—and that purpose is fulfilled, completely.

This year will mark the tenth of such Conventions, and as such, it will be even more important than usual. It will be held in Chicago over Labor Day weekend—convenient for everyone, and at a time when even those who can't take time off from work will still be able to attend. There is no reason for not attending, and every reason to be there.

For further information, write to Box 1422, Chicago 90, Illinois. And while you're at it, why not include a dollar for a Membership Card in this Tenth World Science Fiction Convention? You'll get a deed to a crater on the moon—but you'll also get the genuine satisfaction of knowing you've helped to insure that this will be the best Convention of all. The people working on it have all been donating their time and effort, and the least we can do is to support it with our Membership Dollars.

The Convention Committee will be happy to give you any reasonable help in planning your trip, incidentally, and Chicago is a city that is ideal in accommodations and entertainment.

Personally, we wouldn't miss it for a deed to the whole moon! We'll hope to see you there.

SPACE SCIENCE FICTION

The Editors

NEW MEDICAL EVIDENCE SHOWS HAIR CAN BE SAVED!

Hair-Destroying Germs Disclosed

Shown above are germ organisms believed by many leading medical authorities to cause seborrhea and dandruff that may result in hair loss and eventual baldness.

"Kill these scalp germs," say these doctors, "and you remove this *cause* of itchy scalp, dandruff and seborrhea, ugly head scales and unpleasant head odors — and stop the hair loss they cause."

LABORATORY TESTS PROVE GERMS KILLED BY SEBACIN

Exhaustive tests* made by a nationally-known impartial testing laboratory prove conclusively that Sebacin KILLS ON CONTACT all of the hair-destroying bacteria named by leading medical authorities as a significant cause of baldness.

Sebacin was tested on cultures of staphylococcus albus, corynebacterium acnes and pityrosporum ovale on 1-minute exposures. The test method was the F.D.A. wet filter paper method described by the United States Department of Agriculture.

Sebacin killed the test cultures on contact.

**Report No. 4967, May 31, 1949*

MEDICAL AUTHORITIES BLAME GERM INFECTIONS FOR COMMON BALDNESS

TESTED AND PROVED by men and women all over the U. S.

"Like many others, I had very little faith in your product, but after using it I can earnestly say I was amazed, for it has done wonders for me and I assuredly recommend your product to anyone with falling hair." *A.A.—Oakland, Calif.*

"My husband has used a bottle of your formula and it's done wonderful results for his scalp and hair. So I'm sending for the treatment for myself." *Mrs. V.A.—Hannibal, Mo.*

"On January 28th, I received my scalp treatment and that evening I got busy with it. From the first application and up to this day I have had no itchy scalp. And I cannot comb a hair out." *R.S.—Pittsburgh, Pa.*

"Have tried many hair tonics, but your treatment is the only one that has proven satisfactory." *C.B.W.—Lynchburg, Va.*

"Got rid of my dandruff." *R.H.McD.—N. Kansas City, Mo.*

"Had despaired of ever having normal head of hair again. Getting wonderful results from your treatment." *Mrs. M.B.—McKeen, Pa.*

"Stopped my scalp itch and been wonderful for my scalp." *A.R.—Belle Fourche, S. D.*

"Received great relief from itchy scalp and dandruff from your treatment. I find it has stopped my falling hair." *A.K.—Randolph Field, Texas*

"My hair seems to be growing since I started using the treatment. People around here have noticed the recent results. I'll tell you it's wonderful." *Mrs. J.R.—Jacksonville, Texas*

"I am sure delighted and really satisfied with the results. My dandruff and falling hair have stopped altogether." *J.T.—Stockton, Calif.*

Washington, D. C. — New hope was offered to men and women suffering from the age-old problem of baldness, in recent testimony here by leading dermatologists.

Beware of these 5 danger signs

Neglect May Lead to Baldness

1. **Over-dryness of hair and scalp**
2. **Scalp Itch**
3. **Hair loss**
4. **Dandruff or seborrhea**
5. **Excessive oiliness of hair and scalp**

Most people lose a few hairs daily. This is no cause for alarm as they are immediately replaced by the normal, healthy scalp. However, when you see any or all of the danger signs listed above, it is often a warning of scalp infection and approaching baldness.

Grateful users of Sebacin Basic Formula write that a single treatment will often eliminate annoying symptoms. By keeping the scalp clear and free of germ infection, you give nature a chance to replace hair loss.

In revealing statements, it was disclosed that specific bacteria are invariably found in seborrhea and dandruff, and may be the *cause* of these scalp conditions which result in baldness! The dangerous scalp bacteria named were the staphylococcus albus, the microbacillus or corynebacterium acnes, and pityrosporum ovale.

In reply to direct questions, the medical authorities agreed that:

1. At least 50% of doctors and dermatologists experienced in treating hair and scalp disorders are convinced that seborrhea and dandruff are an important cause of baldness.
2. This baldness may be *prevented* if seborrhea and dandruff are controlled.
3. The bacteria staphylococcus albus, the microbacillus or corynebacterium acnes, and pityrosporum ovale are invariably found when seborrhea is present and are considered to be its cause.
4. An antiseptic containing b-hydroxynaphtholene, sodium phenosulphonate, cinnamic acid and other specialized drugs can and *will* kill these germs.

This impressive testimony by competent medical doctors now made public for the first time, offers renewed hope for the treatment of sick scalps and the prevention of baldness.

Absolutely Nothing Known to Medical Science Can Do More To Save Your Hair!

At last offered to YOU is a revolutionary formula series based on the most recent medical knowledge of hair and scalp problems.

It's great news for those who are impatiently waiting for a treatment to help eliminate dandruff and seborrhea, scalp itch, dry hair, and to stop the hair loss they cause.

Read the facts on this page, the medical testimony, the laboratory report on how Sebacin kills

the hair destroyers—the microbacillus, the pityrosporum ovale, the staphylococcus albus —*on contact!* Read what grateful users from all over the United States write about the Sebacin treatment.

Then study our guarantee. You are the only judge. Remember the Sebacin home treatment must accomplish for you what it has for all the others—or the full cost of the treatment—every nickel—will be returned to you.

Maybe you're among those who have tried every kind of hair preparation until now with no success. Maybe you are skeptical as to whether Sebacin is the preparation you have been waiting for.

Either way, don't delay! You have everything to gain—at no risk. We can state without reservation that NOTHING — ABSOLUTELY NOTHING KNOWN TO MEDICAL SCIENCE CAN DO MORE TO SAVE YOUR HAIR!

Delay may cost you *your* hair! Fill out the coupon and mail today.

Guarantee

The Sebacin formula series is warranted to be made of U.S.P. standard ingredients, compounded under rigid scientific conditions. The Sebacin treatment must result in marked improvement to your hair and scalp, or we guarantee full and immediate refund upon return of unused portion of treatment.

Sebacin Inc.

(*Clinical samples of Sebacin formulae are available without charge to medical doctors, clinics and hospitals upon request.*)

BALDNESS WON'T WAIT! *ACT NOW!*

SEBACIN INC. 400 MADISON AVENUE, DEPT. SF, N. Y.

Please send at once the complete Sebacin hair and scalp treatment (60 days' supply) in plain wrapper. I must be completely satisfied with the results of the treatment, or you GUARANTEE full and immediate refund upon return of unused portion of treatment.

☐ Enclosed find $10. (Cash, check, money order). Send postpaid.
☐ Send COD. I will pay postman $10.00 plus postage charges.

Name...

Address...

City............................ *Zone*........ *State*..............

APO, FPO, Canada & Foreign — no C.O.D. 31-A

MAIL NO-RISK COUPON *TODAY!*

CAPTAIN FUTURE
WIZARD OF SCIENCE
COMET
FICTION AND FACT OF THE PRIZE-RING
FIGHT STORIES
THE BLACK UHLAN
HEADQUARTERS DETECTIVE
MURDER TREADMILL
G-MAN JUGGERNAUT
MASKED RIDER WESTERN
BORROWED HOSSES
FIGHTING ACES OF WAR SKIES
WINGS
10 STORY WESTERN MAGAZINE
ADVENTURE NOVELS
Thrilling Stories of the Sky Trails
AIR STORIES
THE NIGHT HAWK
GEORGE BRUCE
AIR WAR
CAPTAIN DANGER OVER MACASSAR STRAIT
THE ALL-STORY
WARLORD of MARS
ARMY Romances
BASKETBALL STORIES
GAWKY of GUARD
Battle Stories
O'LEARY IN ACTION IN ETHIOPIA
All Star Issue of Favorite War Authors
BLACK BOOK DETECTIVE
GOLDEN FLEECE
HISTORICAL ADVENTURE
ROMAN HOLIDAY by TALBOT MUNDY
HIGH-SEAS ADVENTURES
THE SEA ROGUE
ADVENTURES OF THE FIRST AMERICANS
INDIAN Stories
BRIDE of the TOMAHAWK PACK
MY LIFE WITH SITTING BULL
April
LONE RANGER
MAGIC CARPET MAGAZINE
PEARLS FROM MACAO
MARVEL SCIENCE STORIES
THE TIME TRAP
NEW DETECTIVE
NO BODY BUT YOU
North-West ROMANCES
GIRLS of WHITE WATER TRAIL
Oriental STORIES
PHANTOM DETECTIVE
DIAMONDS
PLANET Stories
QUEEN OF THE MARTIAN CATACOMBS
A BIG CASEY NOVELETTE by GEORGE BRUCE
POPULAR DETECTIVE
DEATH IN A COTTAGE
MURDER INSURANCE
PRIVATE DETECTIVE
NOV 15c
LOVE STORIES OF THE REAL WEST
RANCH ROMANCES
Maid of the Valley
STORIES OF WESTERN AVENGERS IN ACTION
RANGE RIDERS
SIX-GUN VALLEY
Vice Squad DETECTIVE
25c
SECRET of the HOUSE of HORROR
TOP-NOTCH STORIES ... TOP-NOTCH WRITERS
UNDERWORLD DETECTIVE
FIVE FATAL MINUTES
KILLER BAIT
THRILLING WONDER STORIES
THE FEDERALS IN ACTION
G-MEN
GOVERNMENT GUNS
THE BLUE LOTUS
GIVE 'EM HELL
SCIENCE FICTION
PLANET OF THE KNOB HEADS
15c
JULY
SPICY-ADVENTURE STORIES
HELL'S RIVER

www.ingramcontent.com/pod-product-compliance
Lightning Source LLC
LaVergne TN
LVHW090953080826
845145LV00003B/989

* 9 7 8 1 6 4 7 2 0 5 5 8 4 *